Trinity's Trust

Book Five of the Sawyer Brothers Series

C.A. Harms

Trinity's Trust

Second Print Edition: August 2018

Limitless Publishing, LLC
Kailua, HI 96734
www.limitlesspublishing.com

Formatting: Limitless Publishing

ISBN-13: 978-1-64034-963-6

Prologue

I thank God every day that I was stranded along Henry Lane, sleeping in my car. Or Michael's car, I should say. An old silver Corolla that I was surprised to find got me as far as it did.

When I first met Michael, I had been young and naïve. Looking for that one big break that would take me away from all the heartache in my life.

Marrying him was a spur of the moment decision I regretted every day since. But at the time, he made me feel like I had been rescued from a life of uncertainty. I met him when I was twenty-one years old and had no real stability in my life. My mother had abandoned me for the drug addicted life she led. Yeah she was there, but only physically. I'd practically been on my own my whole life. I'd bounced around from place to place living with random friends, or some nights I was even forced to sleep on the streets.

That was until I met Michael Westerfield, a twenty-eight-year-old man from Dillon. He had a long record of battery and abuse he neglected to tell me about, so I had no reason to fear him. I was young and blinded by the possibility of a life I had only imagined, a life full of things I'd only dreamed of.

A man to love me, a roof over my head, and food on the table. Laughter and comfort, with complete support.

I was in desperate need of security and when he made me feel he could offer that, I fell hard for his lies.

Then he flipped the switch and the life I had been living on the streets was something I found myself wishing I still had.

Now here I was, almost seven years later, and I still found it hard to believe I had the life I had now. The love that surrounded me every day was a love most only dream of. I had been adopted into the Sawyer family as if I had always been a part of it. All three Sawyer men treated me as their younger sister, and Tammy was the most amazing woman I knew. She was the glue holding all of us together. Family was everything to her, and in turn it was everything to us.

I had the friendship of Amber, Bailey, and Alena unconditionally. And our sweet Olivia was the sister I never had but always wanted. She was my best friend regardless of our age difference.

They accepted me.

They loved me.

And I would be forever thankful for the joy they'd each brought into my life.

Even if that joy came with three men who watched over me like hawks, stalking their prey and just waiting for one man to make the wrong move.

They were ridiculous at times, but I secretly loved their hovering; it made me feel safe.

But I'd never tell them that.

Chapter One

Trinity

Sometimes I woke from a dream of still being trapped in that house, still fearful of his anger. My mind would fall back to that place where I felt it was all deserved. Michael had a control over me I couldn't explain, and I allowed it to continue for far too long.

I lived with it and just accepted it as my fate until that final day when I could no longer take the hate he showed me. I could barely even tolerate myself because I was so shameful of my life and how far I'd let things go.

It was my fault I never stood up to him; instead, I allowed him to knock me down daily and take all his anger out on me. He had a way with words that could make anyone feel inferior to him. He was condescending and manipulative and I was a fool.

It was disgusting, the person I had become.

I was really heartbroken now when I thought back on it all. How I'd wasted precious time, time

I'd never get back.

But I escaped and somehow, by some miracle, I found my way to Livingston. I stumbled upon some of the greatest people with the warmest souls. And I was proud to refer to those people as my family. It didn't matter that we didn't share the same bloodline; they loved me just the same and I in turn loved and adored them. It was because of the Sawyer family that I found the strength to press charges against Michael for the things he had put me through. It was because of them I filed for divorce and started to once again live my life.

I would forever be grateful to Noah and Ryan for helping me find the right path that day. They honestly could have shipped me down the road and forgotten about the homeless girl they found stranded in a car on a back country road. Instead they introduced me to the women they loved, and in turn I found myself surrounded by so much joy I had no idea what to do with it all.

The three Sawyer men referred to me daily as their sister and so did their wives. And Tammy, God bless her, gave me the love of a mother, something I'd never had before, and nothing had ever felt so good.

It was something I treasured and in no way could I ever explain just how thankful I truly was.

The bond we'd formed could never be broken. I was finally home.

I had become so wrapped up in my own thoughts I hadn't heard the bell above the door of Sassy Ladies chime, announcing a customer had entered. But at the sound of a deep voice just a few feet behind me, I yelped in surprise as I spun around with my hand pressed tightly against my chest.

There, only a few feet away, stood the man who'd starred in so many of my dreams lately. So vivid and convincing that it was hard not to feel they were real.

Chase Douglas.

The new guy in town. Or not so new anymore, considering he'd been in town for well over a year.

He was so god-damn yummy, but there was no way I could even tell him I thought so. But I sure allowed my mind to race off with in-depth thoughts of the things I would love to do to him.

"Sorry to scare ya," he said with a smirk.

He'd transferred to the Livingston Police department when a position opened up. He was the grandson of Mrs. Willard, the crazy old lady who reported my car along the road when I first found my way to town. She was the woman most avoided because she was anything but friendly. Most feared her, or the idea of her. I'd heard all about the times she'd pulled a shotgun over the years.

But recently her health had taken a turn for the worse, and with Chase being the only remaining family she had still willing to offer help when needed, he came to be close to her.

You'd never guess this perfect, sculpted, yummy as hot fudge on a sundae, topped with all the cherries and whipped cream a girl could handle, man came from the same blood line as Mrs. Willard, but he had. She was his mother's mom. Now I didn't know the complete details of his family, but I had been told it was a little messy. And if anyone knew what messy was like, it was me.

"You okay?" His question snapped me out of my fantasy yet again.

God, he must think I'm some kind of freak.

"Um, yeah," I said, clearing my throat and attempting to regain some form of control. "Is there something I could help you with?"

I watched as his eyes lowered toward the item I was currently twisting mindlessly around in my hands.

The moment I shifted my gaze downward my mouth instantly went dry.

It had to be a thong.

And not just any thong, but a bright red, lacy, see-through thong.

I felt my cheeks heat as he traced his lower lip with the tip of his tongue, slowly bringing his eyes upward to once again meet mine.

"I was just putting the new line of lingerie out," I said, trying to take the uncomfortable feeling away. I should have stopped there. But no, I had to keep spewing shit out like each word would somehow fix the situation I found myself in.

Note to self—talk less, breathe more.

"We have these in eight different colors with matching bras and garters. Plus these new nighties that the women in town seem to love." He just continued to watch me, without saying a word, which only made my mouth keep moving and my heart race even faster.

"They sell much better than the last brand we had. They were a bit itchy and the material snagged, eventually leaving holes in the product."

In that moment I wanted to just turn around and walk away. I was without a doubt a rambling fool. And the way he was just looking at me with that damn grin of his told me he, too, found this situation to be one laced with humor.

Only I wasn't laughing; I was mortified by the way I had allowed myself to run my mouth off.

He reached out and pulled the panties from my hand. "I didn't come here to shop for…lacy thongs. But just so you know, I'm not opposed to having you model them for me." He smirked and I felt my stomach drop. I swear it hit the floor at my feet.

Was he seriously flirting with me?

"I came in to ask if you'd be interested in going to dinner, with me?" He still held the thong in his hand as he moved his thumb over the silk material.

My mind wandered off once more, to the idea of him continuing that very movement over and over, only this time when the panties were tightly hugging my body. I felt my core clench as I imagined the way it would feel as his hands ran over my hips and along my thighs.

"Should I take your silence as a no?" he asked and I panicked suddenly.

"No," I said a little too loud and he chuckled. "I mean yes. Or wait a minute. No, my silence doesn't mean no, and yes, I'd love to have dinner with you."

Oh my God, I was such a dork.

"Okay." He smiled wide and placed the silky material back in my hands, only this time he didn't pull his hand away. The movement from earlier, the one I had allowed myself to fantasize about, was being repeated. Only this time it was my palm he was rubbing.

I tried not to pant, but it was seriously one of the hardest things to accomplish. I had the urge to climb this man like an oak tree or rub up on him like a cat. He was so damn good looking and he smelled amazing too.

"Tomorrow night?" he asked, and like the idiot I was, I only nodded. "Six thirty?" And yep—I nodded again. He chuckled again. "I'll pick you up just across the way; I know where you live."

Apparently Mr. Douglas had been paying attention. That thought sent chills over me as he turned around and walked toward the front door of Sassy Ladies.

Never had a pair of slacks made a man's ass look as good as they did Chase's. I bit my lip to keep from moaning and when I noticed that sweet ass was no longer moving I looked up to meet the knowing smirk of the most handsome cop I knew.

Yep, I'd been caught admiring his ass.

Another mark on the embarrassing moments tally board.

Chase Douglas was dangerous to my libido and my sanity. He had my mind racing and my body heating and we hadn't even gone on a date yet.

I was definitely in for a world of trouble.

Chapter Two

Chase

I walked out of the small boutique with a smile on my face. A smile that made my cheeks ache.

I'd been observing Trinity for some time.

I liked to watch her when she didn't know I was doing so.

I loved the way her eyes lit up whenever she was surrounded by the Sawyer girls. So many times I wandered out of the police station and found her in the small park just across the street, her golden hair flowing in the breeze while she was lost in her latest paperback. I would find myself just admiring her, getting lost in the moment.

She was beautiful.

But she had no idea just how appealing she was.

I didn't know every last detail of her past, but I did know a few things. One thing I was sure of was she had this kindness about her that made my chest ache.

Each time I'd see her act silly with one of Ryan's

boys, every single smile she shared with Jackson's little girl, it just gave me one more chance to witness the beauty she held inside.

Beauty that some asshole tried to diminish.

But then she would pull back just a little, as if the sadness in her tainted every moment of happiness she was gifted.

Like she felt that happiness was something she didn't deserve. Or she didn't know just how to accept it.

I hated to see that sadness.

But now I was done watching from afar. I wanted to know her more. I wanted to find the ache in her and heal it.

Replace all those sad memories with nothing but good ones.

Call it the hero syndrome, call it whatever you want. But I called it seeing something I wanted, and finally growing tired of wanting from the sidelines.

It was time I went after what I wanted.

I was going after the girl.

I'd spent months surrounding myself with only two things.

Work and Nana.

They both took up most of my time.

But I needed something more. I needed something for me.

My family deserted Nana after a huge fallout over my grandfather's will.

Who did that kind of thing, anyway?

Who walked away from a woman who had just lost her husband, who had no one else to turn to, over money and items she was entitled to? All things she and Grandfather built together.

Greed was an ugly thing.

I was ashamed of my parents, and I refused to turn my back on her like everyone else did. One day they'd regret their actions, regret their harsh words.

But in the midst of all the crazy, thinking of Trinity always made me smile.

Hell, her little nervous behaviors and the uncontrollable ramblings—I'd never seen anything more sweet.

I'd sat back and observed long enough. I was ready to get to know the real Trinity.

I had a feeling this girl was going to take me on one hell of a crazy ride.

And nothing excited me more.

***

"Chase, I need my walker," Nana's weak voice hollered from the other end of the hall. "And my teeth," she added with a cackle.

She did it every time.

The woman knew that specific thing was my weakness. Hell, I don't know why, but there was something god-awful about retrieving a set of teeth, soaking in some type of cleaning solution, from the ledge above the sink. I swear the woman did it just to torture me.

And this was just one of the many reasons I needed a life outside of Nana and the station.

I was a twenty-nine-year-old bachelor living with my grandmother. The most exciting thing in my life right now was *The Walking Dead* on

Sunday nights with Nan.

Pathetic, I know.

I walked into the living room carrying a walker in one hand and the entire bright blue container, with the solution still inside holding a set of false teeth, in my other hand.

Ignoring her sly grin, I held the container out, refusing to watch as she reached in and pulled the teeth out herself. My stomach turned and my throat constricted as the liquid from the container sloshed out onto my hand. I tried to think of anything else other than the fact that I was now wearing remnants of my Nana's slobber and whatever else had been floating in that water on my hand.

That shit was like acid burning through my skin. At least that was how I envisioned it. It was taking everything inside of me to ignore the way it ran over my wrist.

And when I reached the point I could no longer ignore it, I bolted.

Moving like lightning I dropped the walker, spun on my heels and practically sprinted to the kitchen sink, Nan's laughter following me the entire way.

Tossing the container to the side, I grabbed for the soap and began scrubbing my hands over and over until my stomach settled and I could no longer envision the horror I had just felt.

Nasty, god-awful things had happened to me since I moved in with Nana.

Things I was sure would forever haunt my soul.

I looked back over my shoulder and found her smiling brightly from the entryway.

Something told me the woman lived to torture

me. She looked entirely too pleased with herself.

People said she had a mean streak.

Hell, I've heard some horror stories over the months, not only from family but from those around town.

But I'd say she's more ornery than mean. At least to me anyway.

She was bullheaded, set in her ways, and damn it—she wouldn't back down for nothing. The woman got her way, no matter what it took.

And she didn't give a second thought to those she pissed off along the way.

To me she was tough as nails and I admired her.

Hell, with all the shit she faced from the family that should have been supporting her, she had the right to be stubborn.

I adored the woman, scowl and all.

Chapter Three

Trinity

"You need to breathe." Alena looked at me with an amused look. "He asked you out because he's interested. That part's done. Now just sit back, relax, and be yourself."

Was she crazy?

Be myself.

The woman hadn't witnessed my word vomit yesterday. If she had, she wouldn't be telling me to be myself.

"I'm gonna say something stupid," I assured her as I turned around to look at myself in the mirror.

"You'll be fine," she said. "And this dress looks amazing on you, so even if you do, he'll be too focused on these legs of yours to notice."

She'd been playing dress-up with me all afternoon. After I told her about Chase asking me out, she broke out the new line from some top designer friend of hers and I immediately became her new dress-up doll. Not that I was complaining about having the most gorgeous dresses at the tips of my fingers, though—I was in awe.

There I stood in a form-fitting dress flared out at the bottom and in the most amazing shade of blue.

I did look good.

I smiled at my reflection in the mirror just as the bell above the door chimed.

I spun around expecting Amber because she'd already said she was coming over to do my hair, but she wasn't alone.

If it had only been Ryan tailing behind, I would have just shrugged it off as no big deal. On most days he was easy to handle. Hell, all ya had to do was threaten him with Amber and normally he backed off pretty quick. A trick I leaned from Olivia.

But he had an accomplice.

Jackson.

Why he had been the one to claim fatherly duties when it came to me, I was still unsure. But when more than one Sawyer man came at ya at once, they were so much harder to tame.

"So were ya planning on sharing the news about your date with us?" Ryan leaned against the countertop as Amber rounded the end and moved toward me with a bag of hair products and a curling iron.

I couldn't help but giggle when she rolled her eyes.

"Didn't see a reason to clear it through you," I said with a shrug, choosing to ignore the scowl he wore.

I could see the reflection of both men in the

mirror in front of me and neither of them looked too impressed with my brush-off.

"Well, it's all good," Jackson said with a smirk. "We cornered your boy at the station this morning."

I turned around so fast I knocked the bag Amber was holding out of her hands and the contents spilled to the floor.

"What do you mean you cornered him?" The images rolling around in my mind had me on high alert. Nothing about Jackson and Ryan cornering Chase was giving me warm fuzzy vibes.

"We just made it perfectly clear how important it is, to his health, that he chooses to act like a perfect gentleman in regards to you," Ryan stated proudly and Jackson chuckled.

The looks the two of them were exchanging had my stomach coiled in knots.

Embarrassment at its worst filled my chest and I instantly wanted to call the whole thing off.

"Relax," Ryan added, giving my now racing heart no further comfort. "He knows right where we all stand now. It's all good."

I wanted to clobber the both of them.

Now I knew exactly what Olivia felt when she first brought Keeton around. That poor guy spent weeks over summer vacation trying to prove himself to the Sawyer men, and even then he still struggled.

I could only imagine how much of an outsider he felt, and now it appeared Chase would be forced to face some of the same things. The problem was he and I hadn't even gone on our first date yet.

These arrogant asses were gonna scare him off

before I even got the chance to see if the fantasies I'd had held a candle to the real thing.

They were interfering with my need for male contact, and I thought it might be time for them all to realize they just didn't do that to a woman who had spent entirely too long with a set of batteries instead of the real thing.

"If you two torment Chase to the point where he changes his mind about me, I can assure you you'll see a whole side of me you never knew existed." I glared at the two of them, daring them to say even one word.

Amber laughed and Alena leaned against the counter, her arms crossed over her chest as she smiled wide.

It was funny to watch Ryan and Jackson share a look of confusion. It was like they were debating on pushing me further, wondering if I would prove my point.

"We just don't want to see ya hurt, Trin." Ryan was the first to speak. "You know we love ya, and us not taking our chance at warning a guy about the expectations we have…well, we can't let that slide. It's not in our nature."

"Well I can assure you both that though I adore you for attempting to save me from any future heartache, I can handle it." I loved them both for wanting to protect me, but there was no reason for them to hound Chase when all the guy had done was ask me out.

"It is just one date," I told them and both of them remained in the same position, watching me. "I've been here in Livingston for close to seven years.

And I've never been happier. I'm not the same girl you all found sleeping in her car along a back country road. I'm stronger, and that's because of all of you. I can assure you if Chase, or any other man for that matter, gets out of hand, I won't stand back this time and let it happen."

"Neither will we," Jackson said without hesitation.

"The first man to try would be signing his own death warrant," Ryan grumbled and I couldn't help but laugh.

"Okay," I said through my laughter. "Now can the two of you stop being so damn nosy and let us do the girly stuff?"

Chapter Four

Chase

I walked into the kitchen feeling anxious about my date with Trinity, especially after the interrogation I had gone through that morning.

Ryan and Jackson Sawyer made it a point to assure me that Trinity was their sister, blood or not. If I hurt her, that gave them the right to set me straight.

Now I could smile about it, but I didn't dare then.

I knew the connection Trinity had with the Sawyer family. It sure as hell didn't take a damn genius to see that they all adored her.

I came to a halt when I found Nana bracing herself with one arm on the counter while she balanced a stack of bowls on her other hand.

"Woman, what are you trying to do?" I hurried to her side and braced her with my hand on her back.

The lady was no more than one hundred pounds

and weak from all the medications and other hell she'd gone through. Yet none of this stopped her from doing things that made my damn heart stop.

On more than one occasion I thought of tying her ass to her recliner while I was at work for fear of coming home to find she had fallen when attempting something she shouldn't.

Telling her to wait for me to get home was like talking to the old spruce tree in the front yard.

Pointless.

She'd do it anyway and smile, knowing that it was something I disagreed with.

Again, the woman was stubborn as hell.

"I'm fine," she insisted, swatting my hand away as she climbed back down off the step stool she'd used to reach the bowls. "Quit acting like I'm crippled, boy."

"You're gonna give me a heart attack is what you're gonna do." I shook my head, realizing she had obviously made several trips up on that stool within the last hour.

While I was taking a shower and getting ready she was scaling the countertops.

"Where you going all dressed up?" she asked, ignoring my comment.

"I told you I had a date," I reminded her, and she looked back at me with a stern look written all over her face.

"Date with who?" she asked.

I had already gone through this with her this morning, but either she didn't remember or she was only using it as a way to push me for more information.

"Trinity Flores," I said.

She continued to stare at me, waiting for more information.

"She works in town at the Sassy Ladies Boutique. Friends with the Sawyers, more like family really." I was hoping something clicked because I was already running late and really needed to get going.

"Is she the girl they found sleeping in her car along Henry Lane?" She looked at me with a skeptical look.

I had already tapped into Trinity's case months ago. I knew all about her being married to some asshole from Dillon. I also knew the prick abused her and she fled when she felt there was no other escape.

Knowing she had lived that type of life only made me want to hold onto her and assure her she should never fear me.

"Yeah, Nan," I said, still lost in the memories of the notes I'd read.

Broken wrist, bruises both fresh and old.

It sickened me, the terror she must have felt.

"Hmm," she hummed as she once again busied herself. "Well, I'm gonna bake some cookies. I haven't done that in a while." I couldn't decide if she just no longer cared or something about me going on a date with Trinity bothered her.

But instead of fishing for the truth behind her evasiveness, I leaned in, gave her a kiss on her cheek, and walked out the back door.

After climbing up into my lifted Ford, I backed down the driveway and headed into town.

***

Blue was a good color. In fact it just became my favorite. Trinity made blue look good.

Damn good.

The moment she opened her door and my eyes locked on that form-fitted dress she wore, hell—my head instantly began to spin.

She looked down, and paused a few seconds before looking back up to meet my stare. "Do I look all right?" she asked.

Was she serious?

"You look damn good," I assured her, and she blushed. So maybe saying, "You look beautiful," or "Sweetheart, you're gorgeous" might have been a better option, but at the moment my brain-to-mouth filter was a little short-circuited.

I honestly loved when her cheeks got all flushed and she smiled nervously. It happened often; I'd noticed whenever she caught me looking at her or the times I found her checking me out too.

"Thank you," she said so softly I almost missed it completely. "I thought maybe I'd overdressed. I wasn't sure what the plans for tonight were."

At that moment I would have been perfectly happy with a sandwich and chips if it meant I got to continue looking at her and that sweet smile of hers.

"I thought we could head over to that bistro on Second." I stepped to the side as she stepped out and closed the door behind her. "A few of the guys at the station mentioned their wives loved the place."

Trinity looked back over her shoulder as she

checked the lock on the door. "Sounds great," she offered with a smile.

I knew it was wrong, but I was having a real hard time with the thoughts in my mind. They were running off right and left to areas I knew would only get me into trouble.

Thoughts I shouldn't be having this early in the game.

But I had observed this woman for months. It was hard not to imagine the way she would feel in my arms, or the way her lips would feel pressed against mine.

"You ready?" she asked, and I nodded my head as I held out my hand for her. Without hesitation, she placed her hand in mine and I linked our fingers together as I led her toward the truck still idling at the curb.

"That is one hell of a truck," she said, making me smile. "Did you bring a stepladder?" she joked as she paused at the side with her head tilted upward.

Not letting the opportunity to get closer to her pass me by, I stepped up behind her. Placing one hand on each of her hips, I placed my mouth only inches from her ear. "Don't you worry darlin', I'll make sure you get up there safely."

Chapter Five

Trinity

Talk about sensory overload. I had never in my life been more alert than I was at that moment, being that close to Chase.

He was a complete gentleman and held true to his word. He made sure I made it safely up into his oversized truck, and even though his touch was completely innocent, my body didn't get the message.

Chase was sinful. He was so strong and confident, yet there was a sweet kindness about him that made me feel secure.

The Sawyer boys were raised right; they knew how to cherish and protect the women they loved. There was that same gentleness that surrounded Chase in everything he did.

Yet something told me he could be demanding and consuming too.

"How's that ravioli?" I looked up to find Chase watching me, as he held his beer only inches from his mouth.

"It's real good," I confessed, imagining I must have looked like a starved child.

He chose the prime rib and from the looks of it, it too had been amazing. He had devoured it long ago.

"You want to share a dessert with me?" he asked as he lifted his beer and took a small sip.

How one simple question could sound so dirty, I'll never know, but it did.

When he asked me if I wanted to choose, I shook my head, only telling him to surprise me, and in my opinion he chose well.

"Crème brûlée, with only one spoon." He told our waiter just before he stood from his chair and moved to the vacant one next to me.

When I looked over at him with a puzzled look on my face, he grinned. "Just figured it would be easier to share this way."

I knew he'd be dangerous to my sense of control. Hell, before I even knew the guy I was having vivid dreams of him. Even remembering those times I woke up feeling flushed and more turned on than I could ever remember made me feel a little embarrassed.

But having him this close, smelling the spicy rustic scent of his cologne, and feeling the way his jean-clad thigh brushed up against my bare one, it was real hard to hold myself together.

The waiter brought our dessert only moments later and placed it on the table in front of Chase. "Thank you," Chase said, only seconds before he took the spoon in his hand and dipped into the yummy goodness.

I watched in awe as he lifted his arm and turned to face me, holding the custard only inches from my lips. Was he really going to feed me?

"You take the first bite, sweetheart," he said as he grinned and moved the spoon closer.

I didn't hesitate, partly because I was a huge dessert girl. But mainly because I had never had a man who treated me with such care.

The taste was like an explosion in my mouth and I couldn't stop myself from moaning softly as he pulled back the spoon. "That is so good," I whispered.

When Chase didn't answer, I opened my eyes to find him staring back at me with an unreadable expression on his face.

His eyes shifting between my lips and my eyes only made my heart race with excitement.

"You should taste it," I whispered, trying to break the awkward silence.

"That sounds like a great idea," he whispered in return as he reached out and wrapped his hand around the back of my neck, pulling me close.

The moment his lips touched mine, I was pretty sure I sighed. The dreams I'd had of Chase didn't compare to the reality of his kiss. It was so all-consuming; I felt it in every single fiber of my body.

The way he nibbled at my lower lip, teasing it gently with the tip of his tongue, was so erotic.

When he pulled back I remained frozen, with my eyes still closed tightly. My heart raced, and I found it hard not to chase after him demanding more.

"You're right," Chase whispered, and it was then that I opened my eyes and found he was still so very close. He licked his lower lip and smiled back at me. "It does taste real good."

Complete utter meltdown.

It was the only way to explain the way I felt.

I smiled shyly at him and he leaned back, placing some distance between us, but never did he wipe that smile from his face.

He was dangerous, but in the best possible way.

I'd spent the last seven years hiding from the life I led prior to Livingston. I had somehow convinced myself that if I just remained neutral, no dating or attachment, I'd be happy and safe.

I loved the life I led now.

The Sawyers filled my days with such happiness. And though Olivia was much younger than me, she was my very best friend. My life was full of smiles and laughter and I owed it all to them.

But whether I wanted to admit it or not, there was something missing. There was that connection between two people that I'd never felt, but saw every time I was around Ryan, Jackson, or Noah. There was that undeniable love that couldn't be tainted, like between Olivia and Keeton.

I wanted those things.

I wanted a man to look at me like he needed me to breathe. I wanted a man to hold me close and make me feel like there was no one out there that he would rather be with than me.

And whether Chase was the one who made me feel those things, or someone else, I was more than ready to live again.

Or in my case, finally live.

Chapter Six

Chase

I spent my entire shift at the station being berated by not only Ryan and Noah, but every other guy on duty too.

Apparently Trinity had made one hell of an impression on the town folk over the last seven years. She was everybody's sweet girl and it would appear half the town took to adopting her in some way.

I should have left the station in one hell of a bad mood, but nothing could wipe the memories of last night from my mind.

Though she and I may have shared only a few kisses, I felt like they were so much more.

Not once over the last seven years had she dated or even shown an interest in anyone. There was no shortage of available men in Livingston; I thought the population ratio of men to women was completely lopsided. In my opinion, she should have been snagged up right away.

But somehow, by some miracle, she was still available. I was sure some had tried, but I was just thankful it was me getting the chance to get to know her.

So with each question I was asked, each lecture to treat her respectfully that I received, I just kept smiling.

I continued to remember her words when I dropped her off.

I'd love to do this again sometime.

She didn't know I was already planning our next date before we'd even made it through dinner.

Still in my uniform, I pulled my truck into the parking lot next to the bank and walked the half block to Sassy Ladies, smiling the entire way.

I watched Noah's wife, Alena, and Trinity through the front window. Alena was holding up a few articles of clothing as Trinity held a steamer out before them. They'd smile and on occasion laugh at something the other person said.

That smile of Trinity's could light up a room.

After a few more minutes of watching I could no longer keep myself from pushing open the door.

At the sound of the bell, they both turned to face me and I instantly saw the look of shock on Trinity's face.

Alena smiled widely as she turned away, busying herself.

"Hi," Trinity said as she took a step closer. "Did you just get off your shift?"

"Yeah," I replied, reaching out to push back a blonde wave of hair that had fallen from her ponytail. "I didn't wanna head back home until I got the chance to see you."

She blushed as she looked behind her. I looked in the same direction and found Alena retreating toward the back room. Obviously she was giving Trinity and me a little alone time.

When I knew we were alone, I stepped closer and placed my left hand on her hip. "Last night," I began, a little quieter than before. "When you said that you'd like to see me again, I didn't say anything back."

I had wanted to but I was too damn happy. It sort of slipped my mind and I had pulled her in for a kiss instead.

"I wanna see you again too," I whispered, and she tilted her head back and looked up at me. "With me being the only person here to take care of Nana, I just need you to know that though it may be hard for me to see you as often as I'd like, there is nothing I want more than to see where this goes.

"This?" she asked.

"Listen Trinity, I had an amazing time with you," I confessed. "But I already knew I would. I've wanted to ask you out for a while but I had to get everything in my own life settled before I took the chance. And though things are still hectic, as I assume they will always be, that doesn't mean I don't want you around as often as possible."

She smiled, pleased with my words.

"I like you," I said. "I like spending time with you. And I guess I was hoping that maybe you'd be willing to come out to the house for dinner."

"Tonight?" she asked in surprise.

"Yeah, if you're free."

I didn't miss the look of disappointment that washed over her face.

"I can't tonight," she looked down at my chest and my stomach dropped when I started thinking maybe she had another date with someone I might have to scare off.

"I'm watching the boys for Amber and Ryan." I was instantly relieved when she told me her plans. "It's their anniversary."

"Maybe I'll stop by," I said.

She looked up at me, a look of surprise written all over her face.

"If that's all right," I added, and she still looked a little shocked. "What? I like kids." I did.

"Okay," she finally replied. "Just let me clear it with them first."

In my mind I could almost image the steam coming out of Ryan's ears when Trinity mentioned me stopping by his place. Not because he and I didn't get along; we did. It was just different when Trinity was involved. Hell, they all acted as if I was some escaped convict looking to terrorize and destroy the girl.

I was imagining the hoops I would have to jump through in order to prove to them I had no intentions of tormenting her, although maybe I'd just corrupt her a bit. But I had a feeling she would be all in for that part.

"I'll call ya tonight," I told her as I leaned a little closer, my lips hovering over hers. "Have I told you how good you make this dress look?"

And there went the red flush to her cheeks. Damn that look did things to me. The shy sweetness about her made my chest ache.

"No," she whispered. Her hands gripped my waist and she tilted her head back just enough to give me full access to those pouty lips of hers.

"It's definitely not the dress, not at all," I assured her. "It's the woman wearing it."

I wasted no further time before pressing my lips to hers and when she whimpered I pulled her in just a little tighter.

Damn she felt good.

***

I was a human trampoline. Each of Ryan's boys, Rogan and Rory, and their youngest son Ryder, took turns diving off the couch and onto me as I lay on the floor in the center of the living room.

It turned out Amber had the final say in all things Ryan. I made a mental note to remember that detail for future use. There wasn't much he wouldn't do if it made that woman happy.

So for the last hour I'd spent time entertaining the twins and loving every minute of it, even if my ribs would pay for it later.

Trinity sat in the chair laughing as they took turns torturing me, just making it all the more tolerable. Why her laughter gave me such a rush was still a puzzle.

Maybe it was because of her past, or maybe it wasn't. I knew I liked her—she had gained my attention long ago, but there was just something about the way her face lit up when she smiled.

"Okay boys," she said as she stood from the

chair and placed her hands on her hips. Apparently it was time to be a grownup. She played the motherly role well. "It's time to get your jammies on."

All three boys started to protest almost immediately and I was just about to help her out, only I didn't have to.

"Boys," she said and they all stopped groaning, turned toward the hall, and began walking to their room.

"I'm impressed," I said with a smile as I looked back at her.

"I hate doing that," she confessed. "Those sweet little faces looking back at me. The minute they go all sad and disappointed is the worst kind of battle."

I found that hard to believe because I knew this woman's past.

"I just want to cave and say 'Okay fine…let's stay up all night and eat junk food while having the best pillow fight ever.'" She let out a deep breath and I chuckled.

"Those kids love you," I said from my position on the floor.

That seemed to do the trick because her face softened and she smiled wide.

"They are so much fun. Throw Belle, Nora, and little man Billy into the mix and it's the best time." Belle was Jackson's daughter and I'd heard how she was like a little woman trapped in a toddler's body. She kept her parents in line.

"I just hate when I have to go all grownup mode on them."

"We'll have to plan a day with all of them. A day

of fun where we get the chance to act like kids too. We can do all the things their parents refrain from doing, and when we have them all sugared up and wired, we can drop 'em off and be the cool adults they love to be with." It didn't go unnoticed that she looked doubtful for a moment at my words. But it quickly passed.

I pushed up off the floor and moved toward her, weaving my hand through hers, pulling just enough to make her look upward. "I saw the doubt in your eyes." She tried to look away only I didn't allow her to.

"Do you know I first noticed you my second day in town?" She squinted back at me and I smiled. "You were sitting just outside the coffee house on Main Street, and your hair was pulled back in a high ponytail but the wind was whipping it around and you kept tucking it behind your ear. I think I watched you for fifteen minutes from my truck across the street. At that point I figured I should move on before someone thought I was some kind of stalker."

She didn't say anything, just watched me with a look of curiosity.

"Do you think I would've wasted any time at all if my intentions were only for something quick?" I asked not really expecting an answer from her. "I waited to approach you until I got settled. Until I knew that I'd be staying and until I knew that I didn't have anything that would get in the way."

"I noticed you too," she confessed.

"I know." I'd seen her watching me a time or two. "I liked when you watched me," I confessed and she blushed.

"I like what's happening between us," I told her.

"Me too," she replied.

I moved in closer and just before our lips touched, we heard the sound of giggling.

Turning my head to the side I found two boys, one with his pants on and the other holding his in his hands. Huge smiles were on both of their faces as they stared back at Trinity and me.

Two of the cutest damn kids I had ever met.

Chapter Seven

Trinity

It had been three weeks since my first date with Chase. Three weeks of surprise visits to Sassy Ladies from him during his shifts, just to say "Hi."

And three weeks of watching him intertwine himself with my life and interact with the people I loved most.

It was obvious just how hard he tried, over and over, to show them all just how dedicated he was to this relationship between him and me. He didn't let their presence stop him from showing me his gentle side. He didn't shy away from the sweet words he continued to share with me every chance he got.

Chase had three men watching him close, almost always, but it didn't faze him. He didn't falter, instead he took every opportunity to hug me or softly kiss me.

The girls were mesmerized by his kindness and in their eyes he was just the sweetest thing. I had to agree. But the guys weren't convinced yet.

Keeton would coach him along, not that he needed it, but it sure was fun to watch. Keeton had gone through the same form of hazing not that long ago, so he knew all too well what Chase was facing.

But I could see Keeton analyzing Chase too. It was funny how in just a short time being around the Sawyer men he had picked up so many of their mannerisms.

But again, Chase didn't seem to care that they were always watching him. He acted no different.

For days now we'd been recruited to helping Olivia and Keeton. They had been gifted a piece of the Sawyer land and a new home was being built. It was actually a very serene spot—the hill overlooking the biggest lake on the property, and out in the distance you could see the ranch. It was beautiful.

It was also Claire, Olivia's mother's, favorite spot. It was the place where Ryan had married Claire years ago. It was the place Olivia and Keeton planned to marry, and also a place of peace for Liv because there she would always feel close to her mother. She would share the memories she had of that location with her children in the years to come.

Even though Claire was gone, she was never forgotten and I found great beauty in the fact that each person in the Sawyer family felt the importance of her memory.

Never in my life had I ever met such a loving family. Knowing I was a part of it was overwhelming sometimes, but in the best possible way.

"It's good to see that smile on your face." I

looked up to see Olivia approaching with what appeared to be two glasses of sweet tea.

"It feels good too," I added as she took a seat beside me on the old wooden swing.

We sat side by side holding our glasses as we watched the men work. Ryan and Jackson hammered away on the outer wall of the attached garage. Keeton and Chase were working on the trellis that would cover the back porch and Noah—well he was the foreman, or so he thought.

The man was a slave driver.

Maybe he should have considered construction as a career versus a law official.

"Keeton said he's spent the entire morning hearing all about you." I looked over to find Olivia smiling brightly. "It would seem that a certain officer is smitten by you."

I could feel my cheeks heat at the thought of Chase talking about me to the important people in my life. It amazed me that no matter how much the guys tried to intimidate him, it never stopped him from showing his interest.

"He makes me happy, Liv," I confessed as I let my eyes wander back toward the shirtless man who held up a piece of wood while Keeton moved another board out of the way. His back muscles flexed as he positioned the wood over the saw horses before him. "I used to worry that I'd never find anything close to what you have with Keeton, but Chase gives me hope that I will."

"I think you have," Olivia answered without hesitating. "I've seen the way he watches you. The way he smiles when you smile. It's like his one sole purpose is your happiness."

Just then Chase looked back over his shoulder, like he could almost feel that we were watching him. A smile covered his mouth as he winked at me before turning back toward the task of building.

We were taking things slow. I thought due to the harassing tactics of the Sawyers mixed with my own reservations, but Chase just took his time with me. It was sweet, and the pressure was nonexistent.

We were taking our time getting to know one another without the heavy pressures of other things getting in the way.

The time we spent together just felt relaxed, no expectations, no nagging feelings of what should happen next. We went with it, whatever we felt, without thinking twice.

It was a big change of events from my past. For once in my life I felt like I had control.

Chase never once made me feel like what we had wasn't good enough. In fact it was the opposite. He was the sweetest, most gentle man I'd ever met.

From the looks of him, you would expect something much different. Those tattoos and that pretty boy smile of his screamed dangerous. But the only thing he was dangerous for was my heart. I knew with just the small amount of time we'd had together, if he chose to break me, it would be so easy to do.

Chapter Eight

Chase

I'd made the mistake of thinking that stopping by to say goodnight to Trinity while I was still on duty wouldn't be a mistake.

But when she answered the door in those tiny shorts of hers, my control went flying off into the darkness of the night.

Within seconds I had her backed against the wall just inside her apartment and my mouth covered hers in a hungry kiss.

And from the way her body reacted to mine, that needy whimper she gave me each time my tongue touched her in a seductive way, she didn't mind my unexpected visit.

I was on the night shift, which meant there was no possible way we could continue this after I was off work, considering she'd just be getting ready to start her day when I was ending mine.

I knew I should stop.

Everything inside me was screaming out, telling

me I was only torturing myself, but she just felt too good.

When she rubbed her body against mine, I pulled back and looked at her, both of us breathless.

Her lips were swollen from our kiss and something about that made me feel possessive. I liked that sated look on her face, and knowing that I put it there.

"I don't know what made me think this little visit would be easy," I said as she continued to look up at me, panting.

Her chest rose and fell as she tried to control her breathing. The yellow tank top she wore did absolutely nothing to hide her excitement.

"Tonight is gonna be one of the longest shifts of my life," I said with a chuckle.

"Well if you get a chance to sneak away again, I don't mind being woken up by a handsome man in uniform." Trinity bit her lower lip to hide her smile.

She was teasing me.

I'd noticed she'd been growing a little more flirtatious over the last week or so. She tossed in a gesture here and there, making me wonder if it was her way of saying it was time to take things up a notch.

I treaded lightly with her, but not because I wanted to. Hell, I wanted to toss her on the hood of my car and scare the coyotes away by making her squeal, but I held back.

I didn't want this thing between us to end. I wanted it all, so I let her lead. But the problem was Trinity wasn't real aggressive, so I may have been going about this whole thing wrong.

Something told me she wanted more.

"Sweetheart, you would most definitely be worth losing my job over," I assured her.

I could imagine Ryan getting wind of me taking an hour off to get wrapped up in the sheets with Trinity. He'd for sure reprimand me to the hilt if I got caught with my pants down.

"You and I need to plan a night for us," I whispered, leaning in once more to kiss the side of her mouth. "A night without the watchful eyes of those Sawyer boys." I offered her another kiss this time just next to her ear.

She arched her neck, giving me better access to her neck. The response of her body to my touch always set forth a ray of excitement within me.

"Without any form of interruption," I whispered as I kissed along the side of her neck. "Because I'm finding it almost impossible to keep my hands off you."

"Mmhm," she whimpered as I sucked on the delicate skin at the base of her neck.

I pushed my hips against hers, just to show her a little of what she was doing to me, and again she whimpered. This time much deeper.

It felt like my head would explode from the desire to claim this woman fully.

And just as I was about to tell her how much I wanted her, the radio in my car scared us both.

"We have a disturbance at Watson's Pub," dispatch began and I hung my head, doing everything I could to try to bring myself back to reality.

Her laughter made me smile as I pulled back to

look at her. "Oh you think this shit is funny, do you?"

"You got to admit, it is a little funny," she said with a shrug.

***

After my call to the pub, which led to the arrest of two drunken men fighting over a game of pool, I sat in the park just down the road from Trinity's apartment.

I held my phone in my hand and thought of texting her on more than one occasion, but there were no lights on in her apartment. Only the glow of the Heavenly Temptations sign shined just below.

So instead I turned on the radio very low and sat in my idling car, just looking around the small town circle.

It was nice being a part of this community. Everyone knew your name and your business, but if you needed help, generally there were people lining up to do so.

It was much different from the place where I was raised. Though Dallas was a beautiful place, it just wasn't quite as homely to me as Livingston was. I was sure it had more to do with the people who lived there than the actual location itself, but that was because I had a hard time accepting my family after the way they treated my Nan.

And I now knew it had a lot to do with a certain blonde, too.

I still had two hours before my shift ended and as

I'd said, it had been one of the longest in history. But again, I had one woman to blame for that too.

My phone chirped, indicating a message, and I moved to grab it, almost hungry for any form of contact.

I smiled when I saw Trinity's name on the screen.

Trinity: Do you always camp out outside the apartment of the woman you're dating? Or am I one of the lucky ones?

Instantly I looked up toward her place, still showing no sign of her being awake.

Chase: Are you watching me, Miss Flores?

Flirting the way that we did made me feel like a kid again.

Trinity: Maybe I am.

Knowing she was awake made me feel okay about calling her. I'd had enough texting. I wanted to hear her voice.

I wanted to know when she grew excited; I almost craved that breathy whisper of hers.

Chapter Nine

Trinity

My phone lit up with an incoming call, and my stomach did a little flip. I tried not to sound excited when I answered, but let's face it, that was impossible.

"Hi." I couldn't contain my smile. It was almost instant the moment I heard my phone ring.

"Beautiful girl," he whispered. "I've been thinking about calling you for the last couple hours, only I didn't want to wake you."

"Couldn't sleep," I confessed.

"Anything I can help with?" I could hear the hidden message in his question and I couldn't help but laugh.

"Oh, I'm sure there are ways you can help me," I assured him. "But remember, those ways may cost you your job if the wrong people find out."

"Again, I think it may be worth it," he added.

I could picture the smirk he wore so many times, the one that made my stomach tense. It might seem cocky to others, but to me it was more of a boyish grin.

I sorta loved that grin.

"Really, though." He grew more serious. "What's on your mind?"

"I just can't sleep sometimes." I tried to pass it off as a case of restlessness. No big deal, right? Everyone goes through it.

But Chase being the guy that he was just wasn't happy with minimal explanations.

"What's on your mind, Trin?" he asked. "I know you'll say nothing, but I know it's more than just that."

"Sometimes my mind just gets away from me, that's all," I told him. The last thing I wanted to do was talk about my past with Chase. It hadn't been something prominent in our relationship and I didn't want it to be now.

"Bad dream?" He pushed a little more and in that moment I wished I hadn't texted him.

But I also knew there was no way out of this. I wasn't naïve enough to believe that he was completely oblivious to my past. I mean, he could search with the click of a mouse and there wasn't a thing I could do about it.

"Sometimes I dream that I'm not alone," I whispered, instantly feeling foolish. "I know that it's all in my head, but it still doesn't keep the nightmares at bay. But they're just that." I closed my eyes tightly. "Just nightmares, nothing more."

He was silent for a moment and it made my stomach tighten with discomfort.

"I wish there was something I could say or do to

make the dreams go away." Chase's voice sounded strained, as if he was trying to control some kind of emotion. "I wish I'd known you back then, before he hurt you."

My throat felt tight as I tried to swallow past the lump forming there.

"I wouldn't have let anyone hurt you," he stated. "But I can't make that disappear. The only thing I can do is assure you that I'll do whatever I can to make sure no one ever hurts you again."

The seriousness of our conversation had shifted fast. And I knew Chase meant what he said. But I didn't want my past to dictate our future. It was the biggest reason why I never brought up Michael or what happened between him and me. It was exactly where it should be, left in Dillon.

I was no longer that fragile girl; of all people, I needed him to understand that.

"With you I feel safe," I said.

"And that is exactly what I want you to feel," he replied. "The next couple days are gonna be crazy with Nan's schedule, mine, and yours, but soon we need a night for just us. A night that I can spend holding you."

That warm fuzzy feeling I got when Chase went all sweet on me returned, completely overtaking the serious manner from just moments ago.

Chapter Ten

Chase

"Nana," I said in a panic as I rushed toward the spot where she lay on the floor. A tray spilled out before her with what appeared to be what was left of her lunch.

"Oh stop with the fussing," she swatted my hand away as I tried to help her from the floor. "You need to stop treating me like I'm some brittle ole lady."

I bit my lip to keep from telling her that was exactly what in the hell she was.

An eighty-nine-year-old woman, suffering from liver disease and a weak heart. She was still trying to move around the farm like she was in her thirties. She had no regard for her health or her instability. She barely made it two steps on a good day without feeling as if she'd just run a god-damn mile.

The woman was frustrating as hell.

"Will you please just stop being so damn stubborn and let me help you clean up?" I barked in return.

Normally I'd just step back and allow her to help herself, on guard of course, just in case I was needed. With her will to remain fully independent I really had no other choice unless I wanted to piss her off.

But today was different. She'd fallen twice this week already and I had reached my level of patience. The damn woman wasn't going die from the disease and illness that tortured her daily. Hell no, she was gonna die by accident.

I could see the headlines now. Eighty-nine-year-old Winnie Willard falls to her death when she tries to hang a birdhouse from the highest peak of her three-story country home.

I needed to nail all the damn windows shut, hide the ladder, and bolt the front and back doors shut from the outside.

I could swear that since I'd moved in with Nan almost a year and a half ago, I'd aged ten years. She was worse than a damn toddler on a sugar rush.

Her deep laughter shook me out of my anger fueled daze and I looked at her as if she'd lost her mind. "You remind me so much of your grandfather when he was your age." Tears sprung to her eyes and I wasn't sure if it was due to the laughter or if the laughter was just a cover up for her true emotions. Either way I could feel myself choking up at the thought of my late grandad.

"He was always such a damn worry wart. He hovered and barked at me every time I attempted anything on my own." She shook her head, still smiling as if remembering something. "He was a good man." She paused for a moment before her gaze connected with mine once more. "You're a good man."

It wasn't like Nana to get sentimental; she was always so stern, and used her stubbornness as a front to hide behind.

"I don't think I ever told you how much I appreciate you moving here. I know I'm not the easiest person to live with." Fuck, all the damn anger I felt toward her only moments ago quickly faded. How in the hell was I supposed to stay angry at this tiny little spitfire of a woman who had suddenly gone soft?

I knelt down next to her, placing my hand out before her, motioning for her to place hers in mine. When she did, I slowly helped her from the floor and moved her toward the chair to the left.

After she was safely seated, I lowered myself to my knees and made sure she was looking at me when I spoke.

"I have so many memories of this farm. So many memories of you and Gramps." I leaned in a little closer, taking both her hands in mine. "There was never a question in my mind when I overheard your health had taken a dip. The rest of them are just selfish. One day they may wake up and realize their wrongs."

"Yeah well, I got all I need right here," she said as she freed her hand from mine and brought it to rest on my cheek. "Now, son, you need to clean up that damn mess you made."

She smiled and I chuckled, hanging my head and shaking it slightly. The time for softness in Nana had passed. I could remember only a handful of times in my life she went soft. Granddad was always the one I could play well; Nan was the one to call me on my shit.

Always.

"I'll get right on that," I assured her as I leaned in and kissed her on the cheek.

***

I tapped out a message to Trinity and held my phone in my hand, waiting for a response.

It didn't take long for her to reply with the answer I was hoping to receive.

Trinity: I'll be there in ten minutes.

I'd been trying for three days to get her to come out to the house. Each time she'd either been wrapped up with something Sawyer-related or she was too tired after a long day at the shop. Alena had gone to New York to meet with some new vendors and Trinity was working overtime to keep the boutique running while she was gone.

She and I still hadn't quite figured out our schedules and the best way to make them work, but it didn't stop us from trying.

I'd talked to Ryan about changing my shift, but I thought he and Noah still had me on some type of probation when it came to Trin, so they thought it was cute they had that control over me.

Assholes just loved my misery.

It was just after 10:00 when I walked out onto

the front porch to wait for her. Nana had gone to bed close to an hour ago and I didn't expect she'd need me until morning.

I just hoped for a couple of hours where Trinity and I could catch up. I'd found myself missing her like crazy lately. Since Nan fell the last time, I'd been reluctant to leave her side at night, which only made it harder for Trinity and me to see one another.

She'd expressed concern about coming out to the farm; apparently she'd heard some stories about cranky Mrs. Willard that had made her nervous.

But I just kept pushing, reassuring her I would keep her safe. I still found the entire thing funny, how most people in town categorized my hundred-pound grandmother. She'd really given herself a reputation over the years throughout the Livingston area.

But I knew if it came down to it, given the choice, Nan wouldn't hurt anyone.

I'd just finished my beer when I heard the sound of tires crunching along the gravel drive. An exciting rush ran through me as Trinity's rusty Ford Ranger came to a stop just next to my F-250. I chuckled to myself looking at the two vehicles side by side. Hers looked like a tiny Tonka truck in comparison to my own. I swear I could almost fit her truck in the bed of mine.

She climbed out, closing the door as quietly as possible before moving across the yard toward me.

She had on denim shorts that were cut so short the bottom of the pockets in the front hung out and rested on her thighs. And the t-shirt she wore was so snug I could see her belly piercing protrude out against the material. Her hair hung loose, the way I loved, waves of golden beauty.

Damn she was a sight.

"Hi," she said softly, as if she was scared to speak too loud for fear of waking the beast.

I didn't say anything in return, only placed my empty bottle on the small table at my side before standing and moving toward her.

I met her at the bottom steps of the porch and wasted no time gripping her waist and pulling her close. "Hi," I finally said, making her smile. "I've missed you, sweet girl."

Those times she blushed have grown fewer. And in a way that saddened me, because I loved to know that my words affected her. I loved knowing she'd rarely heard the things I told her.

I fed off that shit.

I wanted to be the man who gave her all the things she'd never experienced before.

But knowing she'd finally begun to trust me, that she was finally starting to let me in—that was a good feeling too.

"I've missed you, too," she confessed, pressing her body closer to mine. Her forearms came to rest on my shoulders as she laced her fingers together behind my neck.

The only sounds that could be heard were the chirps of crickets and a gentle breeze that blew the trees surrounding the front of the house. I'd always loved the serenity of this place and right now I was thankful we weren't standing out in front of her place, where any of the town's people could see us.

Because if we were, I wouldn't have done what I did next.

Bending my knees, I hooked her around the back of her thighs and lifted her body from the ground. She squealed and then covered her mouth with one hand as she wrapped her legs around my waist. I held on to her ass, tightly securing her body to mine.

Trinity looked at the house in alarm and I chuckled. "She's out for the night, sweetheart." I assured her, regaining her full attention.

Her mouth hovering only inches from mine, I arched my neck just enough to close the distance.

Over the last week we'd only seen one another in passing, a few stolen kisses here and there, but at this moment there was nothing stopping us. Nothing interfering with what we both felt.

I turned toward the house, our mouths still connected as I moved up the steps.

When I reached the front door, I missed the handle after two attempts and she giggled. "You need some help?" she asked, pulling back from our kiss and giving me a cocky smirk.

I pinched her ass and once again she squealed as she wiggled against me. I used the weight of my body to push her against the door, securing her, to keep her from slipping. "No, I got this," I assured her, pushing my hips forward to show her just what I meant.

She whimpered and when she rotated her own hips against me, my knees grew weak. I looked up at Trinity, her hair falling around her face, her head tilted to the side as she bit down on her lower lip.

I'd never seen anything more beautiful.

"Stay the night with me," I whispered as I once again pushed my hardness against her.

I'd wanted this woman from the first moment I saw her. I'd imagined doing some of the dirtiest, nastiest things to her, over and over in my mind. I'd held onto those thoughts for weeks, months even.

I'd refrained from moving too fast, from taking things too far, because I wanted nothing more than for this woman to know this was more for me than sex.

But I'd reached my limit.

Without even trying Trinity had wound me so tight over the last few weeks and I wasn't sure I could resist any longer.

I wanted her.

I needed her so badly.

"Please say yes," I whispered against her lips as I teased her lower one with my tongue.

"What about…" she began to speak but I cut her off quickly. I already knew she planned to use Nana as an excuse not to take this inside for the night.

"Stay with me," I said once again, much slower this time. I was well aware of the fact that my words now sounded much more like a demand than a question. It was an exact reflection of what I was feeling.

Demanding.

Needy.

And authoritative.

She didn't answer me, only took my mouth in a hungry kiss and I knew in that moment she agreed.

Chapter Eleven

Trinity

My back arched while Chase kissed along my inner thigh as he moved upward.

His warm breath sent chills over my body and I wanted to scream. I wanted to call out his name when his mouth covered my clit, but I knew I couldn't. The last thing I wanted was for his grandmother to catch me in this compromising position.

But holy hell, I was humming with such intense pleasure it was almost impossible to withhold my cries.

"Don't hold back, Trinity," he whispered. "Let me hear it."

Oh, he was cruel.

Or he was a god.

I went with that description because at that moment he had me floating.

I fisted the covers at my side as he gripped my thighs, holding them apart.

His tongue moved over me as if he owned me and in that moment I would have to agree he did. Nothing had ever felt this good.

I was so lost in the bliss of aftermath from his mouth that his movements had gone unnoticed. I expected to open my eyes and see him still positioned between my thighs, but instead found his body hovering over mine as he positioned his hips between my thighs.

With one swift shift of his hips he began entering me as we both moaned in unison.

"Oh," I whimpered. "Yes."

He whispered his pleasure in the form of barely audible curses as he began to move his body against mine. With each thrust of his hips he pulled back ever so slowly to once again repeat his movements, over and over.

And if I thought only moments ago when his head was positioned between my thighs as he feasted on me was heaven, I was wrong. Because the way he moved, the way his face mirrored the pleasure he felt, was complete bliss. Chase knew just how to wring pleasure out of me—mind blowing, toe curling pleasure.

He gave his best, and when I thought there was no possible way it could get any better, he swiveled his hips or did some other trick to prove me wrong.

No amount of dreams or fantasies could have ever lived up to the reality of Chase. He was unbelievable and I was so lost in his world.

Being lost had never felt so good.

***

I woke later than I planned.

Looking over toward the window only a few feet away, I panicked. The sun had risen and I could tell by the brightness of the room that it was well above the trees surrounding the property.

I tried to move but Chase's legs and arms held me hostage to his bed. He was dead weight, obviously still feeling the aftereffects of our night together.

I too could still feel the achiness throughout my body. It was the best kind of ache. An ache I'd welcome anytime.

But no matter how bad I wanted to repeat our events, I had to get out of here. I had planned to be up and gone before the sun rose, avoiding the chances of a run-in with Mrs. Willard.

But by the looks of it, it may have been too late.

"Why you wiggling around, darlin'?" Chase mumbled, still half asleep. "Lie still."

"No," I protested as I continued to try to move out from underneath him. "I need to get going."

"No, you need to stop moving and let me hold you," he said, this time a little more clear.

"I have to get to the shop." It wasn't the only reason I needed to leave but I figured at this point it might be the only one he would listen to. "And I'm already late."

He groaned as he buried his face against my neck. "What if I don't want ya to leave?" he asked, his voice muffled against my collarbone. "What if I want to keep you hostage here with me all day?"

I couldn't control the smile that covered my lips. "Not that that specific thought doesn't send shivers throughout my body, but I just can't."

I heard movement in the hall and I stiffened involuntarily.

Chase chuckled deeply and I swatted at his shoulder. "Damn, woman, she isn't the devil," he said as he pulled back, allowing me a little wiggle room.

I slid from the bed before he could stop me and grabbed for my shirt that was wadded up and lying in the corner of the room.

"Help me sneak out the back," I said as I pulled my shirt over my head and began searching for my panties and shorts.

He laughed again and I shot him an evil glare.

"What are we, teenagers?" he asked. "Sneaking around hoping not to get caught. Hell, why don't you just climb out the window?"

I turned around and looked behind me toward the window, and Chase laughed harder.

"That was a joke," he clarified.

Turning back around I looked at him and tried like hell to gain some control of my racing heart.

"I am not meeting your grandmother for the first time wearing my clothes from the night before and showing obvious signs of doing the nasty all night long." The thought was mortifying.

"The nasty?" he questioned, with his eyebrow arched. I could see the smirk on his face and I wanted to pick up his pillow and beat him with it.

"Stop stalling and get your ass up," I nagged and he did, but not without continued laughter.

By the time I was dressed and sneaking out of his room, I could hear lots of movement coming from the kitchen. Chase trailed behind me still smiling from ear to ear, like this was all some game.

I was just about to twist the handle on the back door and sneak out when I heard the sound I had been hoping to avoid.

"Child, I already know you're here, ain't no use in trying to sneak out the back door." I froze, ramrod straight, and knew my eyes were the size of saucers.

I was terrified and in that moment I did feel like a teenager who had just been caught and now had to suffer the consequences of her actions.

I looked back over my shoulder and found Chase hunched over, holding his stomach laughing uncontrollably.

"With you two moaning and squealing, sounding like a buncha baby pigs all night, there's no way I couldn't know you were here," his grandmother added.

Mortified.

I was absolutely and completely mortified.

Chase laughed harder, to the point where tears were rolling down his cheeks and never in my life had I ever wanted to gut punch someone more. He loved my embarrassment. He was eating it up.

I would never live this down. I knew it.

This scene would follow me forever. And I knew without a doubt it would be used over and over as a form of torture, not only by Chase but every other person I knew in Livingston.

Things like this spread like wildfire.

Chapter Twelve

Chase

The humor in Nana's eyes warmed my heart. She was laying it on thick with Trinity and maybe I should have rescued her, but it was kind of fun to watch her squirm.

It was like a little girl being scolded by her grandma for getting her Sunday dress dirty.

And Nan was like white on rice when the opportunity arose to torment someone.

"So you were really just gonna sneak out the back door and around the side of the house, hoping not to get caught?" She arched an eyebrow at Trinity.

Instantly my girl looked over at me for help and all I offered was a matching questionable stare.

Maybe it was wrong of me to allow Nan to torture Trinity. But something about the gleam in Nan's eyes told me everything would be fine. She just wanted to make Trinity sweat for a bit.

"The last time someone went sneaking around

my house I clobbered 'em with my cane and they spent a few miserable days in the hospital." Nan sipped her coffee as if what she just said was a common act.

Trinity's throat bobbed as she swallowed, still staring at Nana without speaking a word.

"Child, you really are terrified of me, aren't ya?" It was comical the way Trinity's eyes widened just a fraction before she instantly began shaking her head.

"Um, no," she said in a rush. "I'm just truly embarrassed."

"Oh stop with the worrying," Nan told her, finally cracking a smile. "Do you think I never did any of the wild things you kids do today? Hell, I know I've done a hell of a lot worse. I'm no saint."

If she broke out stories of the way her and Gramps used to sneak around doing things I had no business hearing about it would be *me* sneaking out the back door this time.

"I was young once," she said as she zoned out for a minute, deep in thought.

My stomach began to twist with what I knew was coming next.

"Back in those days my late husband and I used to end up in the damnedest of places. The storage closet at the high school, the men's bathroom at that little deli on Main." She made a sound that made my ears ring as she smiled wider.

"Nana," I began to protest just before she got a little grungier.

"And the hood of that ole Chevy of his, out by the lake."

I interrupted with a groan of protest. "Enough," I told her.

She loved to torture me and somehow the entire events of the morning had been shifted to me. Nana found yet another way to get a rise out of me.

Both Trinity and Nan laughed as I faked a shiver and stood from the table, moving toward the coffee pot for a refill.

The laughter from the two of them did make my torment worth it, but I kept my back to the both of them. If they saw the smile on my face, they might consider it an invitation to continue on reminiscing about my grandparents' glory days.

***

I was sitting at the desk just next to the coffee pot, attempting to fill out the paperwork I still had to complete for the arrest I'd made only a few hours before.

Drunk and disorderly. Booker was starting to make this a reoccurring thing. The guy needed a damn hobby. He was still attempting to find the perfect woman; the problem was he was always going after one who was already taken.

That shit never ended well.

"I know that look." I looked up just as Noah sat down in the chair opposite mine. I wasn't sure I liked the look he was giving me.

"What look would that be?" I asked, once again focusing on the papers before me. Sawyers had some type of fifth sense, I could swear it. If you were thinking about it, if it was rolling around in your head, something great, they could almost feel it.

"You better not hurt her," Noah added, which caused me to look up at him once again.

"I'm not that guy; you know me," I said, hoping he could see the honesty in my eyes. In a short time, Trinity had become important in my life.

"No," Noah said, matter of fact. "I've worked with you, yes, but I don't really know you."

He sat there staring back at me, as if daring me to say something different. But I couldn't. It was true. Outside of the station he and I didn't honestly know one another.

"She's had a rough run," he said as he looked down toward his lap. "You didn't see her that day. She was so damn lost and scared. The poor girl actually feared us, like we were going to arrest her, or worse—send her back to him."

Hearing a recap of the day Ryan and Noah found Trinity sleeping in her car pulled at something deep in my chest.

I'd read the paperwork, actually more than once. But seeing the emotions in Noah's eyes made it that much more real.

"Noah," I said, and it caused him to look up at me. "I have no intention of hurting Trinity. I know all three of you, and hell, even Keeton, are all on guard with me, but I mean it when I say she means something to me. I can't sit here and guarantee you that she and I will never have a hard moment. Hell, I bet you and Alena went through plenty of your own."

He nodded and I continued.

"But I can guarantee you that I'll never take her for granted. And never will I intentionally hurt her."

I was on trial.

And I had been for weeks.

But if this was the shit I'd have to go through day in and day out to prove myself, I would.

Trinity was worth it.

Chapter Thirteen

Trinity

"With so much of my time being focused on the house being built and starting my new job at the junior high, the wedding plans have sorta been put off." Olivia looked at me from across the table. "I just realized last night how little time I have left, and how I still have so much to do."

I'd played a part in the marriage proposal between Keeton and Olivia. He used me as a form of distraction so that he could recruit Amber to help him set the entire thing up. Then I was responsible for delivering the girl.

It was all so beautiful and romantic.

I couldn't wait for the day when it finally became official. I knew that no matter what it would be a gorgeous wedding.

"Liv," I said, leaning against the table and reaching out to touch her hand. "The wedding is gonna be perfect," I assured her. "And it's not gonna be that way because of the decorations or the color of the bridesmaids' dresses. It's gonna be because of the two people who have chosen to share their love with the rest of the world."

She smiled, and took in a deep breath.

"It's all gonna be perfect. Because even though you've been busy and Keeton has been focused on the house, everyone else around you has been moving forward with your plans." Amber and Tammy had gone a little overboard with the preparations.

There was no way Amber, or Olivia's grandmother, would allow her wedding to be anything less than perfect.

Ryan was even adding to the mix—because Liv deserved it all, he made sure each person knew that nothing less would be sufficient.

Ever seen Bridezilla in the form of the father?

"So how are things going with Chase?" she asked, pulling me out of my daydream about Ryan with a clipboard and whistle as everyone scrambled around repositioning chairs and flower arrangements. That man was gonna be hell on the wedding day.

Just the mention of Chase's name brought back the events of yesterday morning, and my embarrassing introduction to the woman I had classified as the wicked witch turned out to be fun and quite humorous.

"You're blushing," Olivia pointed out, which only made me feel a strong urge to cover my face. I knew there would be no way around telling her exactly what happened with his grandmother. I was still mortified by the idea she heard Chase and me during our night together. "Spill." She nudged my shoulder with her hand.

I lowered my hands and looked up to find her leaning over onto the table, her elbows resting against the top. The smile she wore was so wide, it made my cheeks hurt. Apparently Olivia needed some juicy details.

Only mine were followed up by some not so juicy conclusions.

Chase teased me for hours after I left, sending me message after message about sneaking out the window next time. The ass was eating it up.

And after I explained it all to Liv, she couldn't hold back the laughter either.

I was that dorky girl, the one who acted first and thought about the outcome later. Had I actually taken the time to think that night and morning after through, none of this harassment would be happening now.

Yet another fail on my part.

***

I was so engrossed in the inventory sheet I was looking over that I had not heard anyone sneaking up behind me. But the moment those strong tattooed arms wrapped around my waist and that familiar masculine smell engulfed me, I just knew it was Chase.

He wasted no time as he pressed his lips to the side of my neck and kissed me before breathing me in. "Damn, I've missed you," he whispered, hugging me just a little closer.

I turned in his arms to face him. I was confused to find that he was already showered and changed out of his police uniform. "I thought you were on shift for another hour?" I asked.

In no way was I complaining that he was done; it just surprised me was all.

"There was a little mix-up with the schedule so I took advantage of the over-staffing." He leaned in and quickly pressed his lips to mine, and I molded against his body.

There was something safe about Chase. When he held me and when he kissed me, I felt like no matter what there was nothing that could touch me. Not if he had a say so.

He gave me a weird sense of security.

His delicate touches, his sweet words, they were things I had dreamed of. Things I had wished for. But they were also things I had convinced myself long ago that I would never have.

I'd believed there were only a few great men out there, and somehow I was the one who always missed out on those men.

Yet now Chase had me thinking maybe, just maybe, I'd been lucky enough to get that chance at happy.

The happy I had seen so many times on the faces of those who surrounded me.

When he pulled back from the kiss he moaned that deep pleased sound I'd heard from him so many times during our night together. It had become a game in my mind, a test to see just how many times I could get him to make that very sound.

I loved that moan.

"How long are you here tonight?" he asked as he traced my lower lip with his thumb. His eyes focused on my lips.

"Until five," I said, pushing my tongue past my lips to catch the tip of his finger.

The action caused him to smile knowingly as his eyes drooped and he leaned closer. "I was hoping I could come over, bring dinner," he said just as he skimmed his lips over mine lightly. He didn't actually kiss me, only teased me to gain a reaction. And of course I fell for it, as I practically chased after him with my own lips.

His deep chuckle broke me from my trance and I tucked my head to hide my embarrassment. Only he stopped me by catching my chin between his thumb and forefinger.

"Do you think you can handle dessert?" he asked with a smirk.

I knew exactly what he was referring to, but had somehow regained my sense of sassiness without my Chase-filled haze.

"I'm sure I can swing by Amber's and grab something she has," I said innocently and he narrowed his eyes. "Any requests?" I asked, hoping like hell that he didn't see right through me.

"Yeah," he replied. "Skip the bakery and go straight home. Because you, Trinity, are the only sweet I want."

I tried to hide the shiver that ran through me but I could instantly tell he noticed.

"Does six sound okay?" I only nodded in response to his question. "Have a good afternoon, sweet girl," he said as he stepped back, still never giving me that kiss I was aching for.

Chapter Fourteen

Chase

I left the boutique feeling light on my feet. It had been so long since I'd felt like things were next to perfect.

Nan had been feeling good, no recent accidents, and her spirits were up. Work was going smooth and the guys had begun to lay off a bit when it came to hassling me about Trinity.

And speaking of Trinity, she was the best damn part of my days. Her smile could warm any heart. And I could see a difference in her, too. She appeared so much happier, not so withdrawn.

She still stumbled about her words more often than not, but that was a cute tic I loved to witness.

Everything finally felt as if it had fallen into place.

I drove back to Nan's with a smile on my face and I bounced my head to the beat of the sound playing loud throughout the cab of my truck. I couldn't even tell anyone the name of the song, but it didn't matter. At this point I was sure any song would be a happy tune right now.

I slowed down at the end of the drive and turned in between the tall trees that fenced the front of Nan's property. When the house came into view, I was surprised to find a silver Challenger sitting in the drive where I usually parked.

Not many people visited us here unless invited, and I knew I hadn't expected any company.

I pulled into the space just beside the sporty car and as I was climbing out of the cab, I practically fell flat on my face. Danielle, the ex I left behind in Texas, rushed down the steps toward me with my best friend Beau only a few feet behind.

Beau was less of a shock, considering the last time Dani and I talked it was more of a screaming match. I was leaving, she didn't want me to, and I left anyway.

It ended with her shoe hitting the tailgate of my truck as I drove off.

So finding her smiling and happy as she practically dove into my arms was a shock.

"Hey handsome," she said, wrapping her arms around my neck. Beau smirked as I stood there with my hands out to the sides wondering what in the hell was going on. "Are you surprised to see us?"

She stepped back, only her hand continued to rest against my forearm.

"You could say that," I said, once again looking back to Beau. "You didn't say anything about coming for a visit."

"Wasn't my idea," he said, pointing toward Danielle. "Dani thought we'd surprise ya."

Like I said, shoe hitting tailgate, which was our final goodbye over a year and a half ago. Now she wanted to visit me.

"Actually I thought it was necessary," she corrected as she smiled back over her shoulder at Beau. And it was the way she smiled at him that made it all make sense. "I thought it was the right thing to do."

Beau still held the same expression, one of seriousness. Dani, on the other hand, had shifted from happiness to a nervous manner.

"It's just that the way we left things and all, I thought it'd be best if we talked to you face to face about something, versus over the phone." I was thankful she finally stepped back and created some space between us.

"You two traveled all this way to tell me that you're dating?" Beau didn't show any signs of surprise at my comment, but of course Dani looked up at me guiltily.

She and I had been together for almost a year before I left. We were close, but in no way were there any wedding bells in our future. She was too dramatic. Everything, and I do mean everything, was made to be a big show. She wanted everyone to notice her at all times and if she wasn't the center of the event, she pouted.

What surprised me about it was that Beau was willing to put up with all that. He and I had talked about her attitude on more than one occasion, and apparently he was now willing to look past it.

"Are you mad?" Danielle's question didn't surprise me. Obviously she was hoping for some type of reaction out of me, a reaction she wasn't gonna get. I never loved Dani, cared about her yes, but it was never anything more than that.

"No," I replied. "I don't have a reason to be mad."

"Oh." Dani sounded disappointed. "I just thought that maybe with our past and…" Her voice faded off.

"Dani, you and I are over; we have been for a long time." I crossed my arms over my chest. "You and Beau dating is completely up to the two of you."

Beau knew me better than most people. He'd known already this would not affect me, but obviously he was attempting to pacify his new girlfriend.

Actually the only thing I truly wanted to offer him was a psych exam, because the dumbass already knew what he was getting himself into but chose to do it any way.

So instead I offered them both a cool drink.

Chapter Fifteen

Trinity

"You got a hot date?" A deep voice startled me as I spun around, holding a box of Amber's yummy caramel brownies, fresh from the oven.

I caught her ten minutes before she planned to leave, and she insisted on making something instead of allowing me to take leftovers from her day.

Ryan stood only a few feet away, leaning one shoulder against the wall, with a questioning look on his face.

"Um, just thought I'd pick up some goodies before heading home," I said with a shrug.

"You do know your forehead scrunches up when you lie." Amber snickered as she continued to clean up the kitchen while Ryan continued to analyze my reactions.

"Not lying," I simply said, as I shifted the weight of my body from one foot to the next.

"Being evasive is the same as lying in my book," Ryan added, still giving me that damn stern fatherly look of his.

Why in the hell did I feel so small when it came to the Sawyer boys? They were just so damn intimidating.

"Oh, you wrote a book?" I looked toward the floor as I attempted to move past him.

Amber laughed, followed by an unladylike snort.

"Quit avoiding the question," Ryan said, stepping away from the wall to block my path.

"Quit being pig headed, stubborn, and an ass," I shot back. I stared at him, narrowing my eyes and hoping like hell he'd back down.

And of course he didn't.

I huffed out in defeat and rolled my eyes.

"Yes, Dad," I said sarcastically. "I have a date."

We continued with some type of weird stare down and I refused to look away. It would have been like basically handing him the winning trophy. This was not a game he'd win.

Did I mention how controlling the Sawyer men could be?

"Is he treating you right?" His question had not been what I expected and I may have faltered just a bit.

"It's still new, Ryan; we're still getting to know one another." Completely true. Chase and I were in the flirty new stages. I knew as well as anyone else that things would shift and change. We'd grow into a comfortable setting where things could and would change. That would be the test to know if we were truly compatible. "Besides I know as well as you that if he wasn't treating me right, I wouldn't be sticking around." I'd learned my lesson in that category long ago.

"Ryan, I thought you were gonna take me to dinner?" Amber said, breaking the seriousness of the moment.

It was like the flip of a switch. That hardness in his features softened and he smiled over at her like she was an angel.

To be loved like that. It made a girl all mushy inside.

"I am, sweetheart," he said in return. "You about ready?"

I wanted to hug her and tell her thanks for rescuing me from the big bad wolf once again, but instead I offered her a wink. She returned the gesture just before moving past me into the arms of her waiting husband, and just one of the three control freaks in my life.

I had always wished for an older brother; never had I expected to end up having three of the most protective ones around.

They were all so impossible.

***

I rushed through my shower, blow-dried my hair, and dug through my closet to find the perfect outfit. Settling on my jean miniskirt and the cutest off-the-shoulder light pink shirt, I dressed in a hurry.

I was so anxious for Chase to arrive that I kept myself busy with meaningless tasks throughout the apartment to keep from looking out the window every few minutes. It had only been a few hours since I'd last seen him, but honestly it felt more like days.

When 6:00 rolled around and Chase wasn't beating on my door, I found myself looking at my phone over and over, wondering if I should worry.

He was the kind of guy that gave you a time and was there fifteen minutes before. He was never late.

When 6:15 rolled around, I sent a quick text asking him if I'd misunderstood and was supposed to come to his place instead.

At 6:30 there was still no response from him and my stomach felt a little uneasy. By the time 7:00 rolled around I was beyond concerned.

I grabbed my purse and keys from the kitchen table and rushed from my apartment, locking the door securely behind me.

The entire drive over I battled with being the overreacting girlfriend, dating buddy, whatever the hell I was to being the nagging girl who had to be thinking we were much more than we actually were.

I slowed at the end of the drive, creeping toward the old crooked mailbox at the edge of the gravel announcing I'd arrived at the Willard farmhouse. For a few seconds I contemplated just driving by and going back to town, but turned quickly to the left before I could convince myself that was the best option.

When I rounded the corner I found not only Chase's truck sitting in the drive, but a silver car too. I hit the brake a little harder than I intended to and jerked forward abruptly.

Suddenly I felt as if the option to drive on by should have been the one I chose.

The view of the front porch was clear and Chase

was not alone. A brunette sat in the chair next to him and a guy with shaggy brown hair sat across from them.

Just as I was about to put my truck in reverse, Chase stood and waved me forward, by lifting his arm up high in the air. The opportunity for escape had just passed.

Chapter Sixteen

Chase

"Who's that?" Beau asked as I walked to the railing that outlined the front porch of the house.

For the last couple of hours I got lost in the old times. Beau and I laughed over the shit we did when we were kids and I'd lost track of how many beers we'd shared between the two of us.

I watched as Trinity pressed on the gas and her small truck began to move forward toward the house once again.

I could feel my body sway a little as the alcohol interfered with my balance.

When her truck slowed to a stop just behind mine, she still hesitated and before I could think twice I was moving toward the stairs.

"That your girl?" Beau hollered out from behind me and I realized I had never answered him the first time he asked.

"Yeah," I said with pride. Because in my eyes, Trinity was mine.

The closer I got, the more anxious I became. Yet she still remained in the cab of her truck looking out through the open window.

I didn't much care for the timid look on her face. It was as if she regretted coming here.

I placed my hand against the roof as I leaned in toward her. "Hey sweetheart," I said, and she flinched just a little. "What's wrong?"

She was silent for a moment as she looked from me to the porch and back again. "I was just a little worried when you didn't show up."

It took me a moment to catch on, but when I did my stomach tightened with irritation. "Shit," I mumbled as I hung my head and let out a frustrated breath. "Baby, I'm sorry."

I felt like a complete ass.

"Beau showed up and I just lost track of time." I began to backtrack, trying my best to make standing her up okay. Only it wasn't; with each excuse I made, I only felt worse.

"It's okay," she insisted, but I could tell her smile was forced. It wasn't the same genuine sweet smile I had grown reliant on. The smile I'd grown to love over the last month.

"No, it's not okay," I leaned in just a little closer and weaved my hand around the back of her neck, her hair getting slightly tangled in my fingers. "I messed up."

"Honestly, it's all right." She tilted her head slightly, leaning into my touch. It eased just a small amount of the tension I felt within my chest. "Why don't I get going and we can just reschedule for another night?" And just like that, the tension returned, only this time it felt multiplied.

"No," I said hurriedly. "Why don't you stay?"

Once again she looked up toward the porch and I could see that she already had every intention of refusing my invite.

"Please," I added, regaining her attention. "I want you to," I assured her.

"I don't wanna impose. I tried to text and then call you earlier when you didn't show up at my place, but they both went unanswered. I was just worried is all." I only felt worse now that I hadn't noticed she was trying to reach me.

"You're not imposing. I want you here." It was then that I took the opportunity to move in closer and press my lips to hers.

I had gotten so caught up in the memories of my past that I'd forgotten all about this sweet girl waiting on me.

"Please stay," I whispered against her lips before kissing her softly once more.

When I pulled back and she nodded her head, I let out a relieved sigh. Things with us were still too new for me to already be screwing shit up. Not to mention I had three men constantly breathing down my neck about not doing that very thing.

Once she was out of the truck I wasted no time linking my hand with hers, and pulling her in close to my side. It had not escaped my attention the way she was watching Dani as I led her up onto the front porch.

"This is Danielle and Beau," I said.

Trinity offered a sweet smile and a soft "Nice to meet you both."

"They're friends from Texas," I added as I unlinked our fingers and wrapped my hand around her waist.

I did my best to make her feel comfortable in the presence of strangers. I sensed that familiar withdrawn demeanor Trinity often used when she was unsure of something.

"This is Trinity," I paused looking directly at her before I continued, "my girlfriend."

She smiled, but just enough to notice before she quickly pressed her lips tight together in an attempt to hide the happiness that very word gave her.

"How long have the two of you been dating?" Dani was the first to speak, breaking the little bubble Trinity and I were lost in. I thought it was a simple enough question and appeared to be completely harmless.

"About a month," Trinity replied. "Maybe a little longer."

"It seems like a lifetime ago that he and I dated." And there went that completely innocent harmless feeling I had only moments ago. *Was that comment really fucking needed?*

"Oh," Trinity said in a whisper. "The two of you were together?"

Maybe asking her to stay was a mistake. I should have just climbed into the passenger seat of her truck and insisted she take me home with her since I'd had too much to drink to drive.

"We fought more than anything, and like she said, that was a long time ago," I clarified, leaning in as close as our current position would allow. "Beau and Danielle are actually a thing now." I felt the dire need to throw that out there.

Dani chose to stop with the unnecessary information. She hated competition. She hated feeling like there was someone else more important than her.

She was so over the top.

I think Beau sensed the discomfort because he took the initiative to start back in on the crazy stories of our adolescence. I made a mental note to thank him later.

Dani pouted, as she watched Trinity closely. But Trin was so focused on the stories being told that she didn't appear as if she noticed being analyzed.

"Well if it isn't the girl who sneaks in and out of my grandson's bedroom." We all instantly looked toward the door, finding Nan standing just on the other side of the screen door with a big smile on her face.

I tried to refrain from laughing, but it was impossible when I looked around at the stunned group. Danielle had her nose wrinkled in a displeased manner and Beau was grinning widely with a smirk. But it was the horrified look on Trinity's face that threw me over the edge.

And when I laughed, she narrowed her eyes at me, as if the threat of her sassiness would stop me.

Only it didn't.

She said she would never live down the fact that Nan caught her sneaking out the other morning and she was right. There was no way Nan wouldn't use it at any opportunity to embarrass Trinity, over and over. She was like a pig in mud when it came to shit like that.

She loved to torment.

"I gotta hear this story," Beau said loudly as he slid forward on the chair and placed his elbows on his knees.

Trinity's head hung low as she turned toward me and buried her face against my chest.

"What's wrong, darlin'?" Beau teased. "It's gotta be a good one if she's so embarrassed she can't even face us."

A loud sigh escaped her and I chuckled. "It was a good one all right." Had I not been half drunk I most likely wouldn't have fed into the tormenting Trinity banter, but I went right along with them. "It was real damn good."

"Oh my god," Trinity whispered. Due to the fact she was still pressed tightly against me, I knew I was the only one who heard her words.

I tilted my neck down and placed my lips close to her ear. "I'm pretty sure you thanked God a few times that night."

Her head shot upward and she looked at me with her mouth hanging open in surprise.

"You did not just say that," she insisted as she looked back toward the other three.

"Oh, he said it loud and clear," Beau said with a chuckle.

Apparently being drunk also made it impossible to whisper.

"If I was a regular church goer, I may have grown offended by your use of the Lord's name in vain that night," Nan added, and within seconds Trinity buried her face once again.

The laughter of Nan, Beau, and I echoed through

the night and I chose to ignore the sour look on Dani's face.

Trinity laughed when I hugged her close and suddenly the weight of the night faded away.

I loved having her here, mixed into my world. My best friend and Nan. Dani was a thorn in my side, but I didn't let her affect the night.

I'd given up trying to please that girl long ago. She was Beau's problem now. And from the looks of it, he didn't give two shits about her plea for attention.

Chapter Seventeen

Trinity

"What do you mean his ex-girlfriend is staying with him?" Bailey asked as she stepped up to my side. I'd not even noticed anyone else was around when I disclosed that bit of information to Olivia.

We were at the park for the annual Fourth of July festivities, at which Olivia and I were named the responsible parties to tend to the grill this year.

I wasn't sure that was the best idea. I was almost positive hot dogs and hamburgers weren't supposed to be crunchy. But what did I know, right?

"Please tell me I heard you wrong," Bailey added, crossing her arms over her chest. "Because I could swear I just heard you say Chase invited an ex to stay at his gran's house with him."

"I wouldn't say he invited her; she just kind of showed up on Tuesday with his best friend from home." I shrugged, trying to play it off like it was nothing.

Did I mention I have a huge inability to pull off

any type of lie? I completely sucked at the faking emotions thing.

"And his ass could have sent them to the nearest motel." Bailey arched her brow, daring me to disagree.

I didn't.

"But she's with Beau, his best friend. They're together, as in a couple, I guess." The words left a bitter taste in my mouth because there was something about the way that girl watched Chase that made my stomach knot up.

"Well, I don't give a shit if she claimed to be a nun. She is his ex." Bailey's face contorted into a scowl. "He should have tossed them a sleeping bag and told them to sleep in the damn barn."

"Who should have slept in the barn?" I spun around to the sound of Jackson's voice and my heart immediately began to race.

I hadn't wanted to bring any of this up to the guys. It wouldn't end well. At least not for Chase, anyway.

But before I could give Bailey a pleading look she went off in true Bailey fashion.

"If you would have ever thought of allowing an ex-girlfriend to stay at your place, I would have hung you from the peak of your roof by your god-damn balls." I heard Olivia snicker and Jackson looked around confused.

"What the hell is she talking about?" he asked me as he pointed toward his wife who was practically shooting flames out of her nose.

"I'm talking about the fact that Chase has allowed his ex to stay at his place while she is in town," Bailey clarified. "I am talking about the fact that Trinity is attempting to convince me that she is okay with it, because, and I quote, 'she's with Beau.' Whoever the hell Beau is. It don't make it right."

Jackson looked back at me and he, too, was scowling.

"As I said they should have slept in the barn, under the spruce tree in the yard, or hell, on the bed of Chase's truck. But the girl surely should not be sleeping under the same roof as Chase."

"It's nothing to worry about," I assured them.

"Oh really?" She crossed her arms once again, cocked her hip out to the side as she looked over my shoulder. "I'd have to disagree sweetheart, because I have seen her kind before."

Everyone turned to look in the direction Bailey was looking and I could have sworn the sound of my hard swallow echoed through the park.

Daisy Dukes didn't even begin to describe the shorts Danielle wore as she walked toward our group, sandwiched between Beau and my Chase.

The smirk she wore as her gaze locked with mine told me she had an idea what might be rolling around in my head.

"That girl right there is trouble with a capital W. And I hate whores." Jackson chuckled at his wife's words.

I was so focused on Danielle that I had not even paid much attention to Chase until he stepped up in front of me, blocking her from my sight.

"Hey, pretty girl," he whispered, giving me a hesitant smile. "Everything okay?"

"Yes," I assured him. But before I could say more Bailey cut in.

"Hell no, everything is not okay." Suddenly I felt like the size of the park had just shrunk. "In fact, nothing about this," she motioned in the direction of Danielle, "is okay."

Danielle huffed and Beau laughed. Not a nervous, what the hell laugh; I'm talking a deep chest vibrating chuckle that also felt as it echoed in the still air.

My guess was he knew exactly what Bailey was referring to.

The relationship between him and Danielle was a weird one. It appeared as if it was one more of convenience than actual feelings.

Poor Chase looked as confused as I was embarrassed. But it wasn't Bailey who hauled Chase off for a little pow wow. Nope.

That would be Jackson, with Ryan and Noah tailing close behind.

Something told me the town fireworks wouldn't be the only loud booms we heard in the park today.

Bailey looked pleased with herself as I gave her a displeased look.

"Really?" I tossed in her direction as I forked the hot dog that was beyond done from the grill and not so delicately shook it free as it flopped onto the platter and rolled to the edge.

The cooler full of beer that Alena was seated upon looked awfully appealing at the moment. In fact snatching it up and finding the nearest dark corner sounded mighty damn fine.

"Let me guess," Beau said with amusement,

regaining my attention. “Those three are the infamous Sawyer brothers I’ve heard so much about over the last few days?”

“Yep,” I offered as I avoided looking up in Miss Sour-Face’s general direction.

“Oh this I gotta see,” Beau said happily as he rubbed his hands together. “I can’t miss Chase squirming like a little girl.”

He rushed off toward the direction the guys led Chase. And that left Danielle surrounded by me, Olivia, and a very annoyed Bailey. I adored the girl but at this moment I wanted to kick her in the shins and tell her to stop giving Daisy Duke the death stare.

I looked up and found Danielle with her arms crossed over her chest, staring back at the three of us as if she thought we should be laying out the red carpet for her arrival or something.

On second thought, Bailey could have at it. Everyone loves a good cat fight once in a while, and Bailey had sharp claws.

Chapter Eighteen

Chase

"Thank God the three of them weren't armed," Beau said with a chuckle. "The big beefy one looked like he wanted to tie you to the back of the nearest pickup truck and drag you through town squealing."

"And you're just loving it, aren't ya?" I said, not even slightly amused.

"Hell yes," he said with a chuckle.

I spun around to face him and he instantly stopped smiling.

"What the hell's going on, Beau?" I asked. "Because you show up here with Dani, acting like the two of you are together, but the whole fucking time you haven't shown one ounce of jealousy when she brings up our past or makes some shitty comment. You know how she is and nothing about this little game feels real."

He looked over my shoulder for a moment before that smile on his face instantly changed.

"She wanted to come alone," he said as his eyes shifted back to mine. "This whole thing between she and I isn't anything more than one drunken hookup. But she made it out to be so much more and insisted on coming up here to share the news with you. I came along to ease the shit-storm I knew she had planned."

"What shit-storm?" I asked.

"I may have shared the news of your dating some girl you really cared for during a game of pool with the guys. Dani was there." He shrugged. "It was also that same night we hooked up and within two days of that night she was ready to take off and share the news with you."

What the hell?

"It never should have happened, but the last thing I wanted was for her to show up here and start shit for you, so I came along to run interference," he added with a shrug.

"You came along to continue to sleep with Dani and play this all out." The guy was a douchebag when it came to women.

"Nah," he said with a shake of his head. "Haven't slept together since that night."

"Not that I truly give a shit, but do you honestly expect me to believe that?" After all, he was Beau, the guy who slept with the mother of one of our high school friends.

"Do you care about this girl of yours?" he asked. Without a moment of hesitation, I replied "Yes."

"Then don't let Dani and her need to be the center of attention screw it up."

"I have no intentions of allowing Dani to screw

anything up between Trinity and me." And that was the truth. I'd not thought once of Danielle until the day I showed up to find her running down the steps of Nan's front porch.

"Then set her straight and send her packing, man. I'll handle the rest," Beau assured me.

The guy may have had a funny way of handling things, but in a way I was glad he chose to come along with Dani. I knew his intentions were good. Dani, on the other hand, had a goal. A goal I wouldn't allow her to reach.

***

"Why are you hiding all the way over here?" She jumped in surprise at the sound of my voice, yet she never turned to face me.

I looked out in the direction she was staring and also became entranced by the sprawling hills and trees.

I felt like an ass. It took Bailey and her sassy ways to point out that I was being an idiot. It shouldn't have taken an outsider looking in to make me realize that Dani staying at my place could only end badly for Trinity and me.

I should have known better.

"She was right, ya know." It was then that she turned to look at me.

I stood with my hands in my front pockets to keep from reaching out and touching her. I still couldn't weigh her mood. For all I knew she was as pissed off as Crazy Bailey.

"I shouldn't have offered to let them stay at

Nan's," I confessed and suddenly I felt like even more of an ass saying it out loud. How had I not seen the wrong in an ex sleeping under the same roof as me?

"I should have known the entire thing between Dani and Beau was just her way of attempting to get under my skin." I hung my head remembering Beau's confession only moments ago. I released a nervous chuckle, before continuing. "She thought it would be a way to show me that I was somehow missing out on her. Hell, I don't really know what her actual plan was, but I know now it wasn't to get my blessing for a life of happiness with my best friend."

I took a step toward her and pulled my hands from my pockets to bring them to rest on her hips, hoping like hell her reaction wouldn't be to knee me in the nuts or shove me away.

When she allowed me to pull her body closer to mine I think I let out a sigh in relief.

"Dani and I were never gonna be long term. Even if I'd stayed in Texas, she and I wouldn't have lasted. She's a bigger pain in the ass than anyone I have ever met." I slouched just enough to line my face up directly with hers, forcing her to see my eyes when I continued. "I waited over a year to go after the girl who almost instantly gained my attention from the moment I arrived in town. And now that I got her, I don't plan on letting her go."

She smiled shyly and hell if it didn't make my chest tighten.

"I don't want today or any other day to be about her," I whispered. "I want it all to be about you and the way you make me feel. Because I'm being honest when I say that no other woman has ever given me that feeling before."

She closed her eyes briefly before looking back at me with a glossiness that wasn't there before. My words had affected her, and that gave me hope that she and I were gonna be just fine.

"This is all still so new between us, but it feels so right." I moved in, bringing our lips closer together. "Every moment with you since that first night has been exciting and fun. I don't want it to end; I just want more."

I gently pressed my lips to hers, trying with everything I had in me to convey what I was feeling through that kiss. It was so slow and natural. A kiss that expressed every word I'd just spoken and so much more I still wanted to say.

And it was the kiss that confirmed what I'd already known.

I was willingly falling for the beautiful wounded girl before me. I wanted nothing more than to show her that everything in her past could be forgotten if she gave me the chance to give her a new beginning.

"Can I stay with you tonight?" I whispered as I pulled back from our kiss and rested my forehead to hers.

"What about Nan?" she asked.

I loved how she always worried about my grandmother and how she, too, referred to her as Nan.

"Well right now she's with Tammy." I smiled when she gave me a quizzical look. "Yeah, it would appear that the Sawyer family has adopted my grandmother, but I'm still on trial."

I chuckled when she closed her eyes for a brief moment and gave a light sigh of annoyance.

Those boys were something else when it involved someone they loved.

"But after the fireworks, Beau's gonna drive Nan back to the house and keep an eye on her for the night." I lifted my hand up toward her face and pushed back the stray piece of hair that had fallen from her braid. "I just want to spend the rest of today and tonight with the only girl who makes my heart race."

And that was exactly what Trinity did.

She calmed me and excited me all at once.

I was a tattooed, buzzed haircut, cop who gave off a badass cocky feel, but inside, this woman made me feel like a lost boy seeking the security only she could give.

It was still so unbelievable how one smile or a simple touch from her could make me feel whole.

"Yes," she whispered. "You should definitely spend the night with me."

She tossed me a mischievous smile and I couldn't help but feel relief that my fiery girl had returned.

I'd been so worried about possibly messing things up between us that seeing her spunky attitude return was exactly what I needed to ease those nerves.

With a nod of my head I gave her another quick kiss before leading her back to the family watching us from afar. I knew without a doubt they'd all been sitting back observing us from afar.

They were like that. Prying and nosy, caring and observant. And deep down, I was thankful Trinity had that type of family backing her up. But they'd better get used to the idea I was gonna be around.

Because no amount of pushing or prodding on their part would ever send me running with my tail tucked. I was in this for the long haul.

They were her people, I knew that.

But I had every intention of becoming one of those people she relied on. I wanted her to love me and trust that I also wanted her happiness. I wanted it all for her, and I would be the one to give it to her.

I'd be sure of that, because nothing had ever been more important to me than her smile.

Chapter Nineteen

Trinity

I relaxed my body back into his as he sat behind me, straddling my hips with his outstretched legs.

His chin rested against the side of my face, as the two-day-old whiskers along his jaw tickled my cheek each time he spoke.

Only a few feet away I'd noticed more than once that we were being watched by prying eyes, only I chose to ignore the hateful glare of his ex. It was easy to see that she and Beau weren't truly in love or even an actual couple for that matter.

They didn't share sweet kisses or gentle touches. Hell, they barely even spoke and somehow I found myself feeling sorry for her. Sorry that she was so wrapped up in her own misery that she might never truly feel the unconditional love of a man who could be out there, somewhere, willing to offer her the world.

I was so lost in thought that when the first firework ignited and scattered throughout the darkened night, I jumped in Chase's arms.

"Don't be scared beautiful, I gotchu," he whispered against my ear, and chills covered my arms and legs as his warm breath tickled my neck.

I arched my neck, looking up at him as a smirk covered his mouth. Without a second thought I lifted my hand up and cupped the back of his neck, pulling his lips toward mine.

I didn't care that every one of the Sawyer men was most likely shooting daggers in Chase's direction. All I cared about was that Chase Douglas did, indeed, have me.

***

I heard his feet against the tiled floor of the bathroom just before he stepped into the shower behind me. Within seconds his body was pressed against mine, and I could gauge his current mood by the part of his anatomy pushing firmly against my ass.

I thought after last night he would be worn out and in desperate need of some recovery time, but apparently Chase bounced back quickly.

He didn't speak a word, only began kissing along the side of my neck as his hands roamed over my wet body.

I could have remained in that very spot, doing that very same thing for hours; he just made me feel so beautiful. It was as if he was using his hands to memorize every dip and curve of my body.

I absolutely loved the way he felt pressed against me, with nothing between us.

When he used his knee to nudge my own apart and pressed his thigh between my legs, I arched my ass, welcoming whatever it was he had planned for me. I craved everything he could offer.

As he stretched his palm out over my lower stomach and began to descend to the apex of my thighs, my body shook with desire. "That's it," he whispered. "Give me what I need, baby."

It was the early hours of the morning with the sun barely up, but if I had a choice of how I'd want to begin every day of my life, this right here would be at the top of my list.

When I felt his cock nudged against my backside, I widened my stance hoping he knew just how much I needed more.

My legs shook with desire. My body quivered with need and any moment I would take charge and reach behind me to guide him where I needed him most, only I didn't have to.

Chase pulled back and with one slow gentle move he pushed inside me and I leaned forward, bracing myself against the shower wall.

He pressed his hand against my lower spine, and I arched my back and began to push against him, meeting each thrust of his hips.

The warm water from the shower hammered over my back and his chest as the sound of our wet bodies slapping together mixed with our pleasured moans.

The moment was so erotic.

It was something I hadn't spent much time missing over the last seven years because no one had ever made me feel the way Chase did. But now that I had it, I would do whatever I had to do to ensure I never lost it.

"You are so perfect, Trinity," Chase appraised me as he continued to move his hips, pulling every ounce of pleasure from me. My legs shook and my eyes rolled as my toes curled into the tile at my feet.

Some women would question the sincerity of his words due to the fact that we were naked in the shower together and he was breathing heavy on my neck, only I had no reason to doubt he was speaking his true feelings. He spoke those same words often, whether we were standing in the shower during an intimate moment or he stood ten feet away looking at me after I just woke up and my hair was sticking out in every direction.

Chase was always telling me I was beautiful, perfect, and the best part of his day. I believed him every time because he made sure of it.

***

Sweat dripped from my brow as it trailed along my cheek before falling from my jaw to land on my bare breast. The fact that it was so hot in the barn I could barely breathe didn't even faze me.

All I could focus on was the half-naked cop who was currently moving his hips at such a fast pace my entire body bounced up and down.

"Yeah," Chase moaned deeply. "Right there, baby." He offered praise as I arched my back and rode out the orgasm that ripped through my body. Within seconds of me exploding around him, his body shook with his own release.

It took what felt like forever to regain my composure as I looked down at the space between us.

Chase remained inside me, using his hips to pin me to the wall and keep me from sliding down toward the floor. His uniform was still on, only his shirt was unbuttoned and his pants had fallen down, getting trapped around the upper part of his thighs.

Somehow I had been stripped of all clothing, and the best part was I didn't remember removing any of it.

"You can surprise me with breakfast before my eight-hour shift any damn day, darlin'." Chase smirked as his eyes looked over my naked body before settling on the place we still remained connected. "Never had a breakfast so damn good before."

I laughed, knowing full well that in no way was he referring to the cinnamon rolls, still sitting untouched on the tailgate of his truck just outside the barn entrance.

What started out as a morning kiss quickly shifted to him tearing at my clothes before lifting me up and pinning me to the barn wall.

"But now you're gonna be late," I said with a smile.

"And it was worth all the shit I'll get for it once I get to the station." He leaned in to kiss me once more. "Nothing is gonna kill this high I'll be on today."

I shifted my hips and he growled as he bit down on my lip, making me whimper. "Keep moving against me like that, sweetheart, and I'll be forced to make you explain to Ryan why he had to stay a couple hours after his shift."

I giggled, imagining how well that conversation would go over.

Chapter Twenty

Chase

"What the hell is that thing?" I tried not to laugh at Jackson as he looked at the ball of fur Trinity held in her arms. "It looks like a fucking rat."

"He is not a rat, you ass," Trinity said defensively as she continued to pet the animal she held.

I wasn't about to admit that Jackson was right, it did look like a rat. A wet, dirty, old oversized rat.

"It's a dog," Trinity corrected and I watched as Jackson's held tilted to the side like he was trying to figure out how on earth that thing she was holding could be referred to as a dog. "I'm not sure what breed he is, but I think he's cute."

"Cute isn't the word I'd choose," Jackson muttered and she shot him another nasty glare.

"He is cute, you ass." She pampered the dog a little more and I swear the damn thing gave Jackson a look of triumph. "What do you think, Chase?"

My stomach tensed and I could feel the sweat

beading on my brow. There were two choices here: speak the truth or take the easy route to ensure my safety.

"I think he's adorable." I chose the safe option.

"Are you fucking blind?" Jackson sneered at me and I almost chuckled at the look of horror on his face. "That thing is so far from adorable. My kids, adorable. A tiny little white bunny bouncing around in an open field, cute." He turned back and pointed at the dog Trinity held. "That thing right there is fucking ugly as hell and needs to be fumigated. It reeks of filth and I think its hair is falling out."

I tried to hold back my laughter, honestly I did. But never had I ever witnessed Jackson in this state. He was confused, and if I wasn't mistaken, horrified by the idea of Trinity calling this dog the same thing he considered his own children to be.

The laughter fell from my lips before I could control it. I hunched over, holding my knees, and my chest shook as I tried to hold it in. Fuck, it hurt my chest. I had tears in my eyes, as I took in one deep breath after another.

"You two are assholes," Trinity said, irritated as she stormed off and I looked up just in time to catch the door of the station slam shut behind her.

I instantly felt horrible.

She showed up at the station proud of the dog she'd decided to adopt after she found it scratching at her apartment door in the early hours of the morning. And Jackson and I just basically told her the thing was damn ugly and resembled a rat.

You'd think we just insulted her child.

I knew I'd have to grovel later to make up for the

damage I'd done, but never in my life have I ever seen an animal uglier than the one my girl had now decided was her new best friend.

When the laughter of both Jackson and I had subsided we both looked at one another, finally registering just how pissed Trinity was when she rushed out of the station.

"You're in trouble," he said, trying his very best to keep a straight face.

"I may be in trouble, but you do know that she's going to call Bailey and tell her you were an ass just as well as I was?" The smirk he was trying to fight dissipated and in its place came a look that spoke "Oh fuck" better than any other expression I had ever witnessed.

A ringing of a cell phone filled the space between us and Jackson reached to his back pocket, pulling his out. And from the look on his face, I didn't have to ask who was calling him. The guy looked like he'd just been kicked in the nuts.

"I better get home," he mumbled as he pushed past me and headed toward the front door.

"Good luck," I hollered out and he flipped me off over his shoulder without offering me a second glance.

Trinity and I had been seeing one another for close to three months now. Over the last month things had started falling into the comfortable state.

Beau had taken Dani back to Texas and a big weight had been lifted from my shoulders. Trinity didn't want to admit it, but she was heavily bothered by her being her in Livingston.

After I made sure Dani understood that there

would never be a she and I, eventually she accepted it. Not without one last plea, which fell flat when I walked away without a second glance.

I know she and Beau were through, if you would actually even consider what they had a beginning.

I knew it wasn't more than a fling that Dani wanted to play out as more.

It was just all part of the weird game she was playing.

But now Trinity and I had hit that stage where bickering over silly things started.

I knew the irritation she felt over the little fur ball she called a dog would be long forgotten later.

Makeup sex was a joyous event.

I couldn't help the smile that covered my lips just thinking about that feisty attitude of hers.

***

The evening was a slow one, and what seemed to make it even worse was Trinity avoided my calls and left the text messages I sent unanswered.

Noah was the worst guy to spend a slow evening at the station with. A person could only handle so much silence before they felt like they were gonna lose their damn mind.

The guy slept.

Yes, slept in the chair while some damn chick show played in the background. Livingston rarely had crazy shit happen. Mostly it was disturbances at the bars on the weekends or the occasional domestic dispute.

When I say domestic dispute I mean two

brothers fighting over the last beer in the fridge. Or a man and a woman who'd been married so damn long they get going at one another, screaming and hollering, which causes a neighbor to call in the law to shut them the hell up.

It was a peaceful community for the most part.

Rosa, the dispatcher who'd worked at the station longer than most of the officers, sat at the front desk, filing her nails. On occasion she would get wrapped up in the show that was playing and she'd freeze mid-file with her mouth hanging slightly open.

Each movement, every sound of the night felt like it was moving in slow motion. Ticking by at the slowest pace, taunting and teasing me.

I could feel the level of impatience rising with each minute that ticked by.

I tried to refrain from looking at the clock, but again it was involuntary. I couldn't stop.

Which only made the damn night worse because again the time was dragging at an unbelievable pace.

When the phone rang I think we all jumped, once again becoming alert enough to realize we still had a job to do, even if it was something as simple as an escaped goat.

I did, however, say a small prayer that the call was not Mr. Fitzgerald calling because Bessy, his cow, broke the fence again.

"Calm down, ma'am," I heard Rosa say as she sat up straighter in her chair. "Alena," she said clear enough that it gained both Noah's and my attention.

Noah moved across the small station so fast he

knocked over a chair in the process and almost face planted only inches from where Rosa sat.

"Honey, is that you?" Rosa asked, squinting as if she was concentrating on what the person on the other end of the phone was saying.

"I need you to breathe sweetheart, I can't…" She didn't even get to finish that sentence before Noah jerked the phone from her hand and held it to his ear.

"Len, baby, is that you?" The worried expression on his face was obvious. "Just breathe, sweetheart, and tell me what's going on. Is Nora okay?"

The idea that something might be wrong with their little girl made my stomach tighten uncomfortably.

Noah was silent for a moment and then something shifted and his concerned stare met mine. There was something in his eyes that instantly made my blood run cold. My heart began to race and before he could say another word I was already reaching for my gun and the keys to the cruiser.

"Just keep her awake darlin'," he said. "We're on the way."

He hung up and began moving toward me. "Dispatch EMTs, Rosa," he hollered over his shoulder. "Tell them to meet us at Sassy Ladies, we have one Caucasian female, unresponsive."

And just like that I felt my world shift beneath my feet.

Chapter Twenty-One

Trinity

2 Hours Earlier

"You're not ugly," I said as I patted his head. "You're handsome." I think I was soothing my own feelings more than his.

Okay, so maybe he was rugged and in desperate need of a bath. But I was sure somewhere deep beneath all the dirt and grime was a cute puppy. He'd been homeless and hungry; I felt terrible about the life the little one had already faced.

"Okay." I patted his head once more before standing. "You have food, water, and a few toys over here." I pointed to each item as if my new friend actually understood what I was saying. "I have to go to the shop for a couple hours and finish some things up. But I'll be back soon," I assured him.

I had fully intended to go back to Sassy Ladies this afternoon and finish orders for the items from

New York that we were running low on. Only after I left the station I brought my new friend Gizmo home and spent the afternoon attempting to clean him up and make him comfortable.

Before I realized how much time had passed, the night had already snuck up on me. I'd actually thought of putting it off until morning, knowing full well that Alena would be okay with it, but I didn't want to start slacking now. I'd never put my work off before and I knew she counted on me.

I owed her.

When the world felt like it was out to get me, Alena accepted me. She gave me a great job, a place to live, and her unconditional friendship.

Plus I knew that most likely Mr. Douglas would be here later this evening after his shift ended to apologize, or bright and early in the morning.

He and Jackson just couldn't resist making fun of Gizmo.

Jerks.

I grabbed my jacket because it was chilly and raining out. After I made sure my apartment was locked up, I moved across the street in a hurry. The rain had picked up and in just the small distance I'd traveled I was already soaked.

Just as I placed my key into the front door of the store, I realized I'd forgotten my phone and the list of items to order on the kitchen table at my place.

I turned around with the intention of going back to get them but screamed out in surprise when I came face to face with a tall man wearing a ski mask.

I had no time to act before he reached out and

placed his large hand around my neck and shoved me backwards against the front door. The handle was digging into my back and I whimpered in pain.

"Don't even think about screaming," he said in an angry tone. "Do what I say and you won't get hurt."

I was terrified.

My legs shook as he unlocked the front door of Sassy Ladies, using my key that he'd taken from my hand.

He was still holding my neck tightly with his other hand; it was hard to breath with the pressure he inflicted.

I tried my best to remain calm as he shoved me backward and I tumbled to the floor.

He didn't turn on any lights, just moved around using the flashlight he held in his hands.

"Where's the money?" he growled as he knocked things over and off displays throughout the room. With each loud crash my body jerked in fear.

"Where's the fucking money?" he said again only louder this time.

When I didn't answer, he approached me in a rush and I began sliding backward toward the back room. He gripped my foot and with one strong tug, I slid across the tiled floor toward him.

I screamed out for help, hoping that someone might be outside one of the other stores in the area, leaving for the night, and that they would hear my cries.

Suddenly, through the darkness my attacker struck out and his hand connected with my mouth. My head shifted to the side from the force of his hit and I could instantly taste blood, a stinging sensation coming immediately after.

"I told you to do what I say," he said only inches from my face. "But you had to make things difficult."

"I'm sorry," I said, hoping to ease his anger.

He grabbed for my hair and yanked upward, forcing me to stand. I yelped out in pain and he only tugged harder.

"Shut up," he threatened.

He moved me toward the register and shoved me forward as my hip caught the edge of the counter. Tears filled my eyes as I fought to hold back my cry from the pain.

"Open it," he commanded.

I watched his shadow through the darkness, wondering what he would do next.

"I said open it," he demanded, moving closer to me.

My hands shook as I tried to enter my code. With each attempt the screen read invalid, which only made him angrier.

"It's in your best interest to stop stalling," he whispered next to my ear, and there was an eeriness in his tone that made my stomach tense even more than it already was. "No one is coming to save you and you're only pissing me off."

Tears clouded my vision. My entire body shook from fear and feelings of terror came rushing back.

After two more attempts, the drawer to the register came open and he shoved me out of the way, hard.

I could hear him digging around, gathering what

money was kept in the drawer. I took it as my chance to move toward the front door slowly, hoping he would be too caught up to notice.

I was so close, feeling a rush of relief that maybe I would be able to free myself, but that joyous feeling was cut short when he reached out and yanked me backwards again by my hair.

"You really can't listen, can you?"

Before I could answer I was hit in the back of the head with something hard and I blacked out.

***

When I came to, I wasn't sure how much time had passed; I just knew that I felt disoriented and nauseated.

My head ached as I tried to push my body up off the floor.

It took a moment for my mind to register what had taken place and that fear of not knowing if my attacker was still inside the store paralyzed me.

I remained perfectly still in the darkness, just waiting for any sign he might still be there.

I could feel the bile rising in my throat as I tried to fight it.

Silence remained throughout the store, giving me the indication I must be alone.

I carefully attempted to slide across the floor toward the desk. When I made it there, I reached up and found the cordless phone.

Each movement hurt my head even more. I'd never in my life remembered having a headache such as the one I had now.

When I tapped at the buttons on the phone I realized that it must be dead, because nothing was happening.

It was hard to hold my eyes open as I tried to look around the room through the darkness. The street light didn't give much lighting to the inside of the store due to the displays covering the front windows.

It took what felt like forever, but I was able to lift my body from the floor and brace myself against the countertop as I moved toward the base of the phone, which held a second handset.

But when I found that it too had no dial tone, I'd then realized the man had ripped the cords from the wall.

I felt the tears sting my eyes when I'd thought of having to move across the road and up a flight of stairs to my apartment for my own phone to call for help. In my current state I could almost guarantee I wouldn't make the trip.

The room spun and I lay my upper body over the counter, just for a moment, in attempt to regain even just a small amount of strength.

I was startled by the sound of the bell above the door, and in an attempt to flee my returning attacker I tried to rush toward the back entrance only to smash against the floor before once again everything went black.

Chapter Twenty-Two

Chase

The front of the store glowed once we rounded the corner on Main Street. Noah insisted on driving, and due to the fear and adrenaline coursing through me, I didn't argue.

But the moment he slowed behind the ambulance parked in front of Sassy Ladies, I leaped out of the cruiser, not even taking the time to shut the door.

I faintly heard him call out my name, but continued to move toward the front entrance.

My stomach hit the fucking floor at my feet when I saw the condition of the store. Things had been thrown around and fallen to the floor. Displays were turned over and items lay broken.

And there in the center of all the destruction lay the woman who I knew held my heart in her hands.

Trinity.

She was unconscious as EMTs worked to secure her on a gurney. A brace was around her neck and blood smeared across her mouth and cheek. Her hair was also matted with blood.

My stomach lurched, as I bent over at the waist, holding my knees. I just needed a moment to breathe; it was all too much.

I wanted to find the person who had done this to her and fucking kill them. I wanted to make them pay.

But losing my shit wouldn't make this situation any better.

I heard Alena attempting to explain what she found, which pulled me back to the present.

"I'd picked Austin from Stacey's place and we were on our way home when I saw the front display in the window tipped over. I pulled up and decided to just come inside and fix it real quickly, but when I put my key in the front door I found it unlocked."

She was crying as Noah soothed her.

"I turned on the light by the front door and that's when I saw her." She took in a deep breath and I looked from Alena toward Trinity, who still lay motionless on the gurney. "She was lifeless."

That's when it hit.

The seriousness of the moment.

I moved quickly toward the paramedics as they lifted the gurney and locked it securely as they began to push it toward the front door.

"Where are the kids?" Noah asked.

"Nora fell asleep and Austin is in the car with her. They're right out front." She followed behind the rest of us as we watched them lift Trinity into the back of the ambulance.

"Call Ryan," Noah said. "Have him send Olivia or Amber for the kids. Tell him we need his help at the store."

"I'm going to the hospital," I said without hesitation.

"Chase, I need you…" Noah began to argue but I didn't let him finish.

"I said, I'm going to the hospital." There was no way I was backing down. I didn't give a shit if I got wrote up or reprimanded; there was no place I'd be other than by her side.

"If that was Alena lying on that gurney, no one would stop you from following right behind and you know it." He stared at me as if he wanted to take on the role of my superior, yet he remained silent.

"I'm going," I said one last time before I climbed up into the ambulance and reached out for Trinity's hand.

I held her hand the entire drive to the hospital as they worked on her. With each second that passed my chest only ached more.

I just wanted to hold her and have her look up at me with those big beautiful eyes of hers. I wanted to see her smile or hear that sweet laugh.

It was fucking killing me that the last time we talked, me and Jackson were giving her shit over that damn dog she found.

***

I paced the hallway for what felt like an eternity. My legs felt as if they each weighed more than a ton, my throat burned, and my head pounded.

Others had arrived at the hospital, also awaiting

any news of Trinity's condition. But all I could focus on was the way she looked when they wheeled her away from me as we entered the hospital.

It took everything inside of me not to demand they let me follow.

I felt so helpless.

Olivia and Keeton, Alena, Jackson even, they all waited.

Bailey and Amber had all the kids huddled at Ryan's place while he and Noah worked to find out who was responsible for the hell Trinity had faced.

Tammy had volunteered to go to my place to sit with Nan, only after we all promised to call with even the smallest of news.

I ignored the pained look in everyone's eyes because it only made it that much harder to hold back my emotions and anger.

Some sick son of a bitch was out there celebrating a small amount of money, while the woman I adored lay in the hospital with injuries I was still unsure of.

"The family of Trinity Flores." I spun around and moved with purpose toward the woman in pink scrubs who stood in the doorway.

"Yes," I said, crowding her space.

She smiled politely and I noticed how she took a step backwards as she scanned over the now large crowd staring at her hopefully.

"Are you all Ms. Flores' family?" she asked with her brows wrinkled.

"Yeah," I said before anyone could speak. "Sisters, brothers," I said knowing that not one of them would argue with me referring to them as such. "And I'm her fiancé."

I'd explain if needed later; for now I would do whatever it took to be included in on whatever she had to say regarding Trin.

"Okay," she said and I felt an instant sense of relief.

She motioned toward a small room off to the side of the waiting area, and we all followed without any further hesitation.

Once we were all inside, she closed the door and turned to face us. "I'm Dr. Jürgens, the attending physician in the ER. I oversaw Ms. Flores throughout her examination." She looked down at the file she held in her hands. "She is very lucky."

"Is she gonna be okay?" Alena asked.

It was the question we all wanted answered.

"She required a couple of stitches to close the cut on her lip. Also, with the impact to the back of her head we also had to add a few staples. She does have a small spot where we had to shave her hair, which I am sure she won't like much." I closed my eyes tightly, thinking to myself if it were a choice between her hair and her life, I'd have shaved her entire head myself.

"I'm unsure of what she was actually hit with, but whatever it was caused a very deep gash. She also suffered a concussion and some minor bruising. The fact that she lost consciousness due to the head injury does warrant some concern, and we'd like to keep her overnight for observation. We'll run another scan tomorrow to rule out any undetected bleeding." Dr. Jürgens seemed very thorough in her examination of Trinity, and that lifted a little of the weight I'd been feeling pressing down on my chest.

"There was a moment of extreme concern when we detected high volume of HCG in her blood, but I can assure you…" I cut the doctor off because I had no idea what in the hell she was talking about.

"HCG," I repeated. "What the hell is that?"

She laughed and reached out, placing her hand on my arm. "It's okay. That's just the hormone all woman produce during pregnancy."

I continued to stare at her wondering what in the hell she was saying. There was no way.

Trinity would have said something, if not to me right away then at least to…

I immediately turned around to look at Olivia and she held her hands up in defense. "I had no idea," she said without a moment of hesitation.

When I turned back around to face the doctor, she was giving me a skeptical look. "Are you saying that none of you knew about the pregnancy?"

I only shook my head, still trying to register the idea that Trinity was carrying my child.

"She's not very far along, maybe six or seven weeks at the most." The doctor continued, only I was so lost in my own thoughts none of her words registered in my mind.

A baby.

I needed to see her. I had to see for myself that she was okay.

I'd deal with the realization that I would one day in the near future be someone's father. Right now I just wanted to touch her, feel her breathe, and know she was okay.

I knew I'd feel better once I heard her sweet voice or even witnessed that smile of hers I loved so much.

"Can we see her?" I asked.

"She's very groggy, but I can allow you to go back for short visits only." Relieved that I wouldn't have to tear into this poor woman for telling me no, I nodded my head in agreement.

"We'll be moving her upstairs once her room is ready, but for now you can go back two at a time."

She thought she'd get rid of me after a short visit. I almost laughed at that thought.

But I'd argue that out later.

Because there was no way I was leaving this hospital without her. I'd hire a nurse to stay with Nan if I had to.

Chapter Twenty-Three

Trinity

They'd given me something for my headache and after what felt like forever the pain had begun to subside.

There was still an aching throb in the back of my head from where the doctor explained I had to have staples to close up the wound, but for the most part it was tolerable.

That nauseated feeling in my stomach remained the same as it had from the moment I woke. The medication they'd given me for that had served no purpose.

But again I would not complain.

Because I was here.

I was alive.

I'd heard horror stories, hell I had lived through some of my own, and I knew things could have gone a whole different direction.

So I was all about counting my blessings.

But that didn't stop things around me from being

hazy. It was almost impossible to hold my eyes open as I dozed in and out of sleep. The sounds of voices were feeding in through my groggy state; they all began to sound the same.

But there was no mistaking one voice.

A deep soothing tone that whispered my name over and over. And that gentle touch that caressed my cheek so tenderly. Even though it hurt my lip to smile in that moment I couldn't control it.

"Chase," I whispered and his lips touched my forehead in a delicate kiss. When he remained in that position as if it was impossible to pull away, I then felt safe.

Completely safe.

It didn't matter that the man who robbed me was still out there somewhere. All that mattered in that moment was the man who remained close, as if he needed to feel my skin against his to register that I was okay.

Because that was exactly what I needed too.

"You scared the hell out of me, sweet girl," he whispered. "When I entered the store and found you lying there as the EMTs worked, I felt like the air in my lungs disappeared. It was almost impossible to breathe."

His confession made my eyes burn with unshed tears.

He pulled back and looked me over as if to finally weigh the damage. "How do you feel, baby?"

"Better now." It wasn't a lie. Having him here made this all easier to face.

Without saying another word, he sat on the edge

of my bed and gently placed the palm of his hand over my stomach. His eyes also focused on that very spot his hand rested.

It remained there for at least thirty seconds before he finally looked up at me with a smile.

"Did you know?" he asked, and I instantly became confused. But before I could answer, he chuckled. "I'll take that as a no."

"Did I know what?" I asked, feeling confused.

"You're pregnant, sweetheart," he replied as he gently moved his finger over my lower stomach. I was shocked, speechless even.

I stared back at him, trying to come up with one full sentence. Something to say in return to this bomb he just dropped in my lap.

Was he crazy? I mean, I think I'd know I was pregnant, wouldn't I?

"No," I said. "I'm not, I can't be. I mean how…" I was just rambling along, trying to come up with some form of explanation.

He just laughed as he leaned forward and pressed his lips to mine. I sagged back against the pillow behind my head while being kissed stupid, only my mind couldn't forget what he just told me.

I was pregnant.

Chapter Twenty-Four

Chase

"We've been through this video a hundred times, Chase." Ryan sounded defeated. "I've looked at every damn angle. The only shot we have is this one."

He tapped the screen, at the frozen picture of the guy who attacked my girl.

"He kept the mask on the entire time. And he kept the lights out, using only the flashlight to move around."

I hit replay as I watched the horrific events that Trinity lived through only three days ago. We had all been spending hours upon hours trying to look for any clue as to who this person was.

Livingston didn't have this type of crime. Hell, most people slept an entire night with their doors unlocked.

But not anymore.

Word got out of the attack on Trinity and people were now in an uproar. Everyone wanted to know.

They wanted this person caught and punished.

But no one wanted that more than me. I wanted this asshole to pay for every ounce of fear he instilled in my girl.

"How's she doing?" Noah asked as he sat down and scooted his chair closer to the monitors.

"Doing okay except at night when she sleeps," I replied as I ran my hand over my face, attempting to wake myself up. "She's restless and wakes up with a jolt all through the night, which only leads to me lying awake next to her just waiting for any sign that she may be having a bad dream so I can wake her before it gets too bad."

Which is what led to my exhausted state. That and the fact I'd been running through video footage of not only Sassy Ladies but the surrounding businesses too. I checked the footage from the bank and the pharmacy, hoping that their outside cameras caught something that would help us in finding this sick man.

I was a mad man on a mission.

I wanted Trinity to feel safe again.

I wanted the town to feel safe.

"I think it's a good thing you convinced her to stay with you while she heals and recovers," Ryan said without taking his eyes of the screen before him.

"She's not going back to the apartment," I assured him, and it was that comment that gained the full attention of both men. "She's moving in with me and Nan."

"Does she know this?" Noah asked.

"She don't have a choice. She can fight me on it

if she wants, but she won't win. The chances of that went right out the window the moment I heard she's carrying my kid." I was completely serious. I knew I'd wanted Trinity long before the news, but now it was sealed. The woman was mine, and there wasn't a damn thing she could do about it.

Noah chuckled as he turned back to the monitor in front of him.

"You gonna do right by her?" Ryan's question gained my full attention. Maybe it was the lack of sleep that made me feel bolder or the knowledge that my child was growing within the woman I would do anything to protect, but I didn't hold back.

"Trinity is mine, the child she is carrying is mine," I said, staring directly at him. "There is nothing I wouldn't do for either of them. So yes, Ryan, I'm gonna do right by her. I'm gonna do right by both of them, and there is not a damn thing anyone is gonna do to stop me."

He stared back at me and for a moment I wondered if I was about to see my superior rip into me. Only he just gave me a pleased nod and as he turned back to the monitor I saw him smile at Noah.

Maybe now these men understood my devotion to their girl, my girl. Maybe they would accept that I would be around for a long damn time, forever if I had it my way.

***

I came home after my shift to find Trinity and Nan in the kitchen. Both woman had their backs to me as they shared a conversation about the best way to make homemade noodles.

I stood back just watching them as Nan rolled out the dough with a rolling pin and Trin watched, fully invested in the task.

"You need to be sure there is plenty of flour, otherwise the dough will stick to your pin," Nan directed as she sprinkled more flour along the dough.

"But does that make it all taste pasty, like flour?" Trinity asked.

"No," Nan immediately replied. "The broth is flavored and seasoned. As you cut the noodles you shake off the excess flour but any loose just helps thicken the broth as it cooks the noodles. And then corn starch will thicken it at the end when we add just what's necessary."

Trinity nodded her head as she continued to closely watch Nan's movements.

I still remember Nan's reaction when I told her Trinity was pregnant. She smiled wider than I think I'd ever witnessed before. "Why the hell you look so damn surprised to find me joyous over the news?" she asked. "I may be a rotten old woman who likes peace but I am a woman. And babies can soften even the hardest of souls, boy."

It was great to see Nan and Trinity together.

I still hadn't shared the news with my mother or father, but when I left Texas, neither of them were entirely happy with me. They felt I'd betrayed them by rushing to Nan's side. Their hope was that if no one came to help her she would cave and give in to all their demands of money and property.

They were selfish people and honestly at this

point I didn't feel they were worthy of the news.

Not one of them had called to check on Nan, or me for that matter, in the last year. So we didn't need their poison tainting our happiness.

"Smells good in here," I said as I finally stepped into the room.

Both woman looked over their shoulders at me and smiled.

"Chicken noodles," Nan announced. "Just teaching your girl here the family recipe. I figure she'll need to know how to make my grandbaby the best when they get old enough to eat the good stuff."

Trinity was still a little thrown off by the fact that she was actually pregnant. I'd accepted it, and had fallen in love with the idea of being a father already. I think I had the moment I heard the heartbeat the day before they let her come home from the hospital.

I knew I'd wanted kids one day, and I knew I wanted Trinity. So what if it was sooner than I'd imagined? Now I couldn't wait to be a father.

***

By the time I crawled into bed that night after getting Nan settled, Trinity was softly snoring. She had been up since I'd left for work that morning before 6:00 a.m. and spent the day helping Nan.

I crawled into bed at her side and she instantly curled her body toward mine, placing her hand on my chest. "You always smell so good," she whispered and I smiled.

"I thought you were sleeping," I said in return.

"How could I possibly stay asleep with you this close," she replied as she opened her eyes and looked up at me.

I brushed her hair back from her face as I took a moment to just look at her. She tucked her chin toward her chest and I continued to watch her. "You are so much more than I bargained for," I confessed, which gained her attention.

"I knew I wanted to know you, that I had to. There was just something about you that no matter how hard I tried to shake it wouldn't dissipate. But never in a million years did I realize I would fall so hard." I let my thumb trail lightly over her lip. The wound was healing and was less sore but it still angered me that she had to face that night.

"I love you," I said as my gaze wandered back to meet hers. I could see the unshed tears that formed in her eyes as she smiled up at me.

"Not just because you're carrying my baby, but that was the turning point that made me realize the love I had for you. It was the moment I truly understood just how much I want you in my life. I want it all with you, the house, the babies, the growing old together and bickering about what to watch on Sunday night television."

She laughed as she blinked and the tears ran along her cheeks.

"I love you," I repeated. "And I love this baby," I assured her as I rested my hand against her stomach.

"I love you," she said in a whisper as her tears continued to fall. "And I want all those things too. But just so we're clear, I get to control what we watch on Sunday nights."

I didn't argue; how could I when she wore that smile? She was happy, so fucking happy. And that was all I wanted. It was what I craved. Her smile, her laughter, it was as if those were the only things of importance with the acceptance of her safety, because never again would anyone hurt her or my child.

That was a promise.

Chapter Twenty-Five

Trinity

"I'm pulling in the drive now," Olivia said through the receiver. "Gran is coming in, and I need to get you to the station. I've already been called three times by Dad telling me to hurry my ass up," she practically growled. "I swear that man is part bear."

I think all the men in our lives were part bear—vicious, dominant Grizzly bears ready to lay down hell whenever it was needed and sometimes when it wasn't.

"Okay," I said with a laugh. "I'm coming out."

I ended the call and grabbed my things as I exited Chase's room and moved toward the living room. "Nan, Olivia is here to get me," I said as I rounded the corner and found her engrossed in her soap opera playing on the television. "Tammy is here for a few hours, so you'll be entertained with cards and gossip."

"Nana loves her juicy gossip," she said with a

grin, still not taking her eyes from the television.

"I'll see you in a couple hours," I assured her.

"Okay Mom," she said, finally looking away from her TV. "I'll be good and stay out of trouble."

She was a feisty little lady and I secretly loved just how she'd accepted me into her life and her home. I never imagined when I first heard of the wicked ole lady Willard that she would one day be one of my very favorite people. But that day had come. I adored her and all her sassiness.

"Don't you try to fool me, Nan." I cocked a brow at her and gave her a matching smirk. "We all know your middle name is trouble."

"That it is darlin'," she chuckled. "That it is."

I pulled open the door and was immediately engulfed in a loving hug from Tammy. I didn't see her nearly as often as I liked to lately, but I swear Chase had me in a plastic bubble. He didn't like that the guy who attacked me was still out there somewhere. Neither did I, but I couldn't keep hiding away.

He would have to accept that one day soon, I would be going back to work and my apartment.

He and the guys still spent hours staring at video after video looking for any clue as to who this guy was. In fact that was what they had me doing, coming to the station to look at some mugshots and video they analyzed. The same videos that have been seen a million times and still they were determined held some piece of information that would lead them to the one responsible.

"How is my sweet girl?" Tammy asked as she pushed back, still keeping her hands on my forearms as she looked me over.

"I'm good," I assured her.

"That boy taking care of you?" She cocked her head to the side. I knew if I said "No" just to be ornery, she would storm off to find Chase and raise some hell. Sometimes I thought Tammy was worse than all three Sawyer boys put together. That woman could get mean when necessary.

"He's taking care of me," I assured her. "He's a good man."

She nodded as she released her hold on me. "Well that's good, because I didn't want to have to get my new nails dirty." She winked. "I would have beat that boy senseless had you said otherwise."

"I know you would have." I surely knew she had no problem telling anyone off who mistreated any member of her family.

"Well you better get going." She looked back over her shoulder and laughed. "Looks like poor Liv is already getting another call from her father."

"Hasn't he figured out by now that tormenting her only makes matters worse?" I thought he loved to fire her up.

"You'd think so," Tammy said, turning back to face me. "I'll see ya later child, I have some stories for Nan I can't wait to share." She hurried past me.

I loved how close Tammy had gotten to Chase's grandmother. The entire Sawyer family, for that matter. They'd all adopted her as one of their own, just like they had me.

***

The ride to the station was filled with Olivia threatening to beat her father for all the hell he'd put her through over the last hour. I tried not to laugh, I truly did, but those two bickered like a couple of old men over a game of poker. It was comical.

When we entered the station, no time was wasted as Chase looked up and noticed me, moved toward me, and wrapped me in his arms.

He didn't kiss me, but just buried his nose in my hair and simply breathed me in. I loved when he did that, because it made me feel treasured.

"You feeling okay?" he whispered near my ear and I nodded my head.

I'd had a little bit of unexpected morning sickness earlier before he left for work. It was the first time I'd experienced it and I could tell he felt horrible for leaving me in that state.

"It didn't last long," I assured him.

"Okay you two, separate and let's look at some scumbags." Ryan sounded so authoritative. Almost like being scolded by a parent.

No one argued as we all moved toward the room at the back of the station. As I entered I looked around and suddenly felt guilty. The room was littered with half empty bags of chips and other assorted junk food. The table at the side held two coffee pots both half full and the garbage can just to the side was filled with Styrofoam cups that had once held numerous ounces of coffee.

They had been working countless hours looking for the guy responsible for hurting me, day after day, night after night. It had just dawned on me that I had not thanked any of them, not even once.

I stood in the doorway as they all moved around the area and got settled.

"Thank you," I said, which caused all of them to look up at me.

"It just hit me that I haven't said thank you to any of you. I didn't thank you for getting me help that night, or for each one of you being there for me while I was in the hospital." I scanned the room as Noah, Ryan, and Chase all watched me. Olivia stood at my side still waiting to join the guys.

"All the hours you've each put in here at the station trying to find even the smallest clue to locate this guy. And I know it didn't stop there because Chase brings it home with him each night, just like the two of you have." I swallowed past the lump that formed at the base of my throat. "Thank you all. I love you guys more than I could ever express and I just wanted you each to know how thankful I am to have you in my life."

Chapter Twenty-Six

Chase

I sat at Trinity's side, with my hand resting on her thigh. I just wanted to be touching her in some way.

We all remained quiet as she scanned over each mugshot Ryan had printed out. Nothing seemed to trigger any memory from that night.

She shook her head as she laid the last of the pictures down. I could sense her disappointment and in some way I felt as if we'd failed her.

"I'm sorry," she whispered and my stomach tensed.

"There's nothing to be sorry about," I assured her as I placed my arm over her shoulders and pulled her in close. "We'll find him."

I wished that I knew that was true, but even I was beginning to doubt myself.

Ryan leaned back in his chair and placed his hands over his eyes as he rubbed at them. He was trying to alleviate just some of the tension I knew we were all feeling.

Noah had his head in his hands as he pulled at the ends of his hair. But when my gaze moved toward Olivia, there was something about the way she was staring at the monitor that made my heart race.

There was a picture of the attacker up on the screen, frozen. It was the only image we had that was remotely clear. When he exited the store and looked back over his shoulder one last time, it was as if the streetlight from outside gave a hue effect from behind him. It highlighted the clothes he wore and his pleased smile as he left behind the woman I loved and the destruction he created.

Olivia tilted her head to the side as she squinted her eyes.

Without saying a word I stood up and moved around the table as I knelt down beside her. "What do you see?" I asked, because I could already tell she saw something she must have recognized.

I heard the sounds of chairs moving against the floor behind me but I remained exactly where I was.

"I can't be sure," she whispered as she moved in closer.

"But you see something," I replied. "Don't you?"

"Liv?" Ryan said, making her jump as she looked back over her shoulder toward her father.

"What is it?" he asked.

There was a moment of silence as she turned back to the computer. "That jacket," she whispered. "Charlie wears a jacket like that."

Ryan and Noah both leaned in close trying to see what she saw.

"That's the jacket all the football players got the year they won the state championship. It was designed for them, and the only difference on each was the number on the right side." She pointed toward the screen. "There is no mistaking that is 00. That was Charlie's jersey number all through high school."

"Are you sure?" Noah asked.

She nodded her head. "I saw him a few days before the attack. He was wearing that jacket," she said with certainty. "I remember because he was flirting with me and it made Keeton irritable. After he walked away, Keeton made a comment about what kind of joker still wore a football jacket from his glory days."

"Charlie?" I asked, feeling completely lost with the conversation.

"Charlie Whitfield," Noah was the first to reply. "He's a kid Olivia went to school with and he's always had a thing for her. She went off to college; he went off to work at the factory with his dad."

"He's stayed out of trouble for the most part until the last couple years," Ryan said, now standing up straight and moving toward the other computer.

He took a seat and began typing on the keyboard.

"He got into some trouble last spring with a group of guys over a bet he'd made, and when he lost he couldn't pay what he owed them. They messed him up pretty bad." Ryan tapped enter and the screen filled with a picture of a younger guy, sandy blond hair. He looked strung out.

"We arrested him later that same spring for possession of a controlled substance and it all went downhill from there," Ryan said as he looked back toward me.

"What do you mean downhill?" I asked.

"Drugs, heavy drinking. Hell, his own father even threw him out after he stole some stuff from him to pay for drugs." Ryan took in a deep breath. "I don't even know where the kid is living these days."

"Well I suggest we start checking around for this Charlie person," I said, standing up and moving toward the table.

I leaned over and kissed Trinity on her forehead. "You have Olivia take you back to Nan's."

I could almost see the argument coming from her, only I didn't wait around to hear what she was gonna say. At that point I had one goal and that was to figure out how the hell to find this Whitfield kid.

He and I had a long overdue chat coming.

***

With Noah driving one cruiser and Ryan driving the other, I and another officer, Raymond, rode along.

We tried Charlie's dad's house first only to find out he hadn't seen Charlie in close to three weeks. He gave us a few possibilities after finally admitting that he'd given up on his son. He was remorseful; you could see it when he hung his head after speaking those words.

"A man can only take so much before he's forced to admit that the help his child needs is well beyond his reach." I made a vow right then that never in my life would I ever give up on my child.

Never.

We came up empty at every place we checked.

The last thing I wanted to do was go home to Trinity and know that once again I had failed her. I wanted to keep looking—hell, I wanted to start knocking on every damn door in town in search of this kid, but Ryan refused.

"There's no reason to work up everyone in town," he said. I disagreed, but kept that to myself.

So after Ryan made it very clear that if I didn't agree to go home and get some rest, he would drive my ass home himself, I gave in.

But it didn't mean I wouldn't be back bright and early tomorrow ready to go again.

Chapter Twenty-Seven

Trinity

I could almost feel the tension rolling off Chase. He was quiet and I often found him staring off to some distant place as if lost in his own thoughts.

I knew he was upset that they had not found this Charlie guy. And if I was honest with myself, I was also disappointed. Not that I thought they hadn't tried, because I knew that was not the case. I knew they had done all they could.

My disappointment came from being ready to put this whole matter behind us.

I wanted to be able to get back to my life and back to the way things once were between Chase and me. He was just so wrapped up in his own thoughts all the time that it made me miss him even though he was right next to me.

"Boy, you need to wipe that scowl off your face." Nan was the first to mention Chase's sour mood.

I watched as he wrinkled his forehead as if to say

she had no idea what she was talking about.

"Don't go playing that game with me. You are one cranky asshole tonight and that girl sitting at your side is just too kind to say anything about it. But we all know already that I'm a sour puss," she said with a smirk. "So I'll say it."

I could see the fiery flame of orneriness burning in her eyes.

"You need to pull your head out of your ass and be thankful for today." I pressed my lips firmly together as I hung my head and waited for Chase to respond.

I was already planning my escape to the safety of the bedroom in my mind.

Two bullheaded people in the same room. One of them in the worst of moods and the other being unwilling to back down. It was a disaster in the making.

"You're right." I looked up in shock when Chase spoke.

He must have instantly noticed my expression because for the first time since he came home from work he laughed.

"I didn't get the result I wanted today, but it shouldn't stop me from being thankful for what I do have," he stated.

I still remained quiet as Nan lifted her body and stood on weakened legs. "Now that I've diffused the tension in the room, I'm going to bed," she said as she started to walk toward her bedroom. "If you'll remember that I may be an ole lady crippled and worn out yet my ears still work fine, I'd be mighty grateful. Because there are just some things a granny should not hear while trying to sleep."

I could hear her laughter all the way down the hall and I knew my face must be red.

When it came to Winnie Willard, she had no boundaries.

She was getting easier to handle, yet sometimes, moments like these, she still threw me for a loop.

"We need to invest in some insulation for these walls," Chase said, which only made me laugh. "At least the walls to our bedroom anyway."

I gave him a skeptical look and he grinned.

"You do know that I have no intention of letting you move back to that apartment, don't you?" He was completely serious. There was absolutely no indication that he was playing around.

"Chase," I said, and he shushed me.

"You're where you belong now. You and my baby are home. There really isn't any reason to argue." And he didn't allow me to. Instead he lifted me up and moved me to his lap where he proceeded to kiss the argument right out of me.

And due to the fact that only moments ago he was broody and cranky, I didn't see any reason to revisit that, not right then anyway. But very soon he and I would have to have this talk, and hash out his expectations as well as mine.

***

How did I get to this moment?

I wasn't complaining, not even a little.

In fact I was so unbelievably thankful that I felt overwhelmed by it all.

Had I thought seven years ago that I'd be where I am now, feeling the way I felt, I would have spent the last seven years counting the moments until Chase found me.

Sometimes, most times, I still felt like it was all a dream.

He was a true southern gentleman through and through. He loved and cared with all he had.

As his body moved against mine, his soft kiss along the side of my neck continued upward toward my ear. Those sweet words of love and pleasure he whispered in my ear only added to the erotic feeling of the entire exchange.

Chase was a very giving man.

Very giving.

"You feel so damn good," he groaned as he pumped his hips a little faster. "Mine," he said in a demanding tone. "All mine."

And I was.

Completely, without an ounce of doubt, his.

I could feel my body reacting to the way he moved inside of me. The spot deep inside that he continued to stroke over and over as he rotated his hips.

"You're so close," he whispered.

I arched my back, threw my head back and he continued to thrust his hips. There was no reason to agree with what he already knew. The man had practically memorized me.

That deep ache inside me grew more intense and my stomach tightened and I curled my fingers in to his shoulders.

"There you go baby," he coaxed me. "Let go."

He trailed his tongue over my ear and pumped his hips faster. "Give it to me, sweet girl." And I did.

My body shook in delightful bliss as he groaned deep in my ear from the reaction of my orgasm.

"Yes," I said in more of a sigh, just before Chase groaned out his own release, burying his face into the crook of my neck to hide it as much as possible.

We really needed to come up with some type of sound blocker. Because this whole attempting to be as quiet as possible during intimate moments was proving to be more and more difficult each time.

Chapter Twenty-Eight

Chase

"We got him," Ryan announced as I entered the station.

"What do you mean you got him?" I asked, suddenly feeling a rush of anger shoot through me.

"Charlie," he clarified.

"And no one fucking thought to call me." I should have known right away. I should have been here when they brought him in.

I pushed past Ryan only to be stopped by Noah when he stepped in front of me to block my path.

"Move," I said.

"Can't do that, brother." He crossed his arms over his chest and showed absolutely no signs of moving any time soon.

"I wanna see him," I said as I stepped up to him.

"That's not a good idea," he declared, only pissing me off more.

"How the hell can you two stand here and protect him?" My hands shook with urgency. I wanted to wring that piece of shit's neck. I wanted to beat him until he was begging me to stop. "You two gave me so much fucking shit when I first started dating Trinity. Hell, you gave me shit for months. Made me jump through hoop after hoop to prove I was worthy, yet the man who hurt her is in that next room and you two want to protect him."

I was disgusted.

How could they do that?

"You think this is fucking easy?" Normally it was Ryan who would have fired back at me, but not this time.

Noah flared up.

The calm, collected, keep the peace man.

He uncrossed his arms and stepped forward, squaring his shoulders.

"Do you think that both Ryan and I didn't have the same rush of anger burst through us when we first heard he was here? I wanted to beat the shit out of the kid and ask questions later." Noah was seething as Ryan stepped up to diffuse the growing tension.

"It's one of the hardest things I've ever had to do, not making him pay for what he did to Trin. No one gets away with hurting my family. But we can't. We took an oath to serve and protect and whether we fucking like it or not, that includes that piece of shit in there too." Noah was always the calm one, so I knew in that moment just how hard this was on them too.

"It isn't to protect him," Ryan said as he stepped up to my side. "I can't let you in that room because it is you I'm trying to protect. You have Trinity and a child to think of. If you're sitting in a jail cell yourself, fighting for your freedom then how in the hell will I explain to Trinity that I let that happen?"

"You've seen the women in our family," Noah said, sounding much calmer than only moments ago. "He'd never survive if he let that go down."

I smiled as I envisioned each one of the Sawyer woman standing before Ryan giving him hell. It eased a small amount of the tension I felt I was drowning in.

"How did you find him?" I finally asked after we had all taken a moment to calm down.

"Garett got a call about 3:00 a.m. from Charlie's father. Apparently Charlie had called him drunk and stoned out of his mind asking him for help." Ryan took a seat at his desk while Noah and I sat in the chairs across from him. "His father knew picking him up and bringing him home wouldn't get him the help he truly needed, so he called the station and gave his son's location."

"He turned his son in?" I asked.

"Yeah," Ryan replied. "He told us that day he knew he couldn't help him anymore. So Garett and Bill went and picked up Charlie and brought him in. He's been sleeping it off in a holding cell since."

"I wanna be in there when you talk to him about the break-in." Ryan instantly began to shake his head no, but I already made up my mind. Nothing would stop me from being there when we read him his rights for hurting the woman I loved. For attacking the woman carrying my child.

"He hurt her," I said, fighting with everything inside me to control my anger. "We may not have known that Trinity was pregnant at the time of the attack, but damn it, Ryan, that asshole could have been the cause for her losing my child. I need to be there."

"I can't let you go off—" he began, only I interrupted him before he could say more.

"I just want see his face when we tell him he's being arrested for his actions that night. I want to witness his tormented expression when he understands that he is going to jail for what he did to her." I took in a deep breath. "I won't touch him, I can promise you that."

Ryan stared back at me for what felt like forever before he finally nodded his head in agreement.

***

My jaw ticked with irritation as I looked the pathetic excuse for a man square in the eyes. He didn't much like me looking at him because he continued to look at his hands folded together on the table before him instead.

He looked filthy and strung out. Obvious signs of drug abuse were all over him. Track marks on his arms, sunken eyes, and rotting teeth. The guy was pathetic.

It took all I had not to leap up from the chair I sat in and wrap my hands around his neck, strangling him as he struggled against me to get even one ounce of air.

I could almost see it play out in my mind.

But Ryan made sure the chances of me getting to Charlie were next to impossible. He not only blocked my path but Noah and Joe, another officer, did too. I was sandwiched between them all with no other choice but to just stare at the son of a bitch who attacked Trinity.

"Where were you the night of August second?" Ryan asked, and Charlie looked up at him with a dead look in his eyes. "And before you decide to tell me some kind of lie, I already know the answer. I already tested the fingerprints we found at the location of a break-in and can assure you that you are a match." Ryan turned around the file that was on the table in front of him and opened it. Just inside was a picture of Trinity after the attack. Her lip was freshly stitched, her eyes were closed and tears were glistening on her cheeks.

I fisted my hands and could feel the anger radiating throughout my body. I shook from the adrenaline coursing through my body.

"So again, I ask you, where were you on the night of August second, around eight-thirty p.m.?" Ryan stared at Charlie, not once taking his eyes off his.

I had to give it to the kid; he tried like hell to hold it together. He sustained eye contact with Ryan, never once hiding his despair.

"I didn't mean to hurt her," he whispered, and it was in that moment I saw fear in his eyes. "I was going through some pretty bad withdrawals. And I just didn't have any other way of getting money for my next fix." He still looked at Ryan as he continued.

"I came around the corner on Main by Mr. Warren's shop and that's when I saw the girl." He shrugged and his lip trembled just slightly as he took in a deep breath. "I just wanted the money, that was all. But when she tried to run, I panicked. I never meant to hurt her."

He then looked around the room at each of us, one by one. Before his gaze met Ryan's once again. "She's all right, isn't she?"

I couldn't hold back. I knew I said I would, but I just couldn't.

"She has nightmares, every night." I tried to breathe in deep to control myself from lunging toward this asshole. "She was lifeless when we found her, and we all stood in the hospital for hours hoping and praying that she'd be okay. While you were out there getting high, she was in the fucking hospital, recovering."

"I'm sorry," he said, now looking at no one other than me. "I truly am."

I believed in redemption. I believed in second chances because most everyone had an ability to learn from their mistakes.

But right then I just couldn't.

Because this was Trinity we were talking about. This man hurt her and no amount of apologies or remorse would ever make me forgive what he put her through.

I knew I could no longer stay in this room. Because if I did I would not be able to hold true to the promise I made to Ryan.

I needed some air.

Chapter Twenty-Nine

Trinity

Olivia spun around so we could all see her in her dress. And she was beautiful, like an angel.

Maybe it was my hormones, who knew, but I couldn't keep the tears at bay.

When I looked around the room I noticed then that everyone else had that same misty eyed look I knew I wore.

"Alena, I love it," Olivia gushed as she smoothed out the silk material that hugged her waist and pooled out just beneath her hips. It truly was a masterpiece. "I've thought about this dress, even envisioned it in my mind. How it would feel, every detail, and this right here," she said as she spun around once again to look at the mirror behind her. "This is so much more than I imagined."

"I'm so glad you love it. It looks amazing on you." Alena looked over the dress, giving off that designer look I knew too well. It was one I'd seen her wear often.

She was analyzing the fit, each inch and every detail. Looking for even the smallest imperfection.

I'd give my left leg if she found one, because I knew she wouldn't. Alena had, over the last few months, spent countless hours perfecting this gown. She was so meticulous with every single stitch.

Anything less than absolutely perfect would not have been accepted in her eyes.

Today was the first day I stepped foot back in Sassy Ladies since the night I was attacked. To say it was unsettling would have been an understatement.

But I pushed forward because I would not let some angry man take away something I loved.

Not again.

This place had always been a place I felt safe. A place I treasured. I wasn't about to let that change.

"I can't believe my little girl is getting married in less than a week," Tammy gushed as she hugged Olivia. "I just know your momma is looking down right now with such love and pride."

That was all it took before the tears began to fall from the eyes of everyone there.

I didn't know Claire, Olivia's mother, but I did know that if she was anything like Olivia, it wasn't a shock how so many people adored her. Olivia had a heart of gold. Sassy, bullheaded, and commanding as the rest of them but the girl was without a doubt one of the sweetest people I'd ever known.

***

When Bailey pulled up in the driveway of the

Willard place to drop me off, both of us nearly had a heart attack.

There on the front porch, perched upon a six-foot ladder, was Nan.

She had a broom in her hand as she swatted it from side to side, reaching toward the peak of the porch.

"What in the hell?" Bailey gasped as she shoved her car in drive and moved quickly. "Belle, baby, entertain Billy," she announced as she hurried off toward Nan with me close behind.

"Woman, what on earth are you trying to do?" Bailey yelled just as she reached the ladder.

"Oh hell, don't you start it too, girl. I hear enough of that shit from Chase," she complained as she lowered her broom. "And that one right there," she motioned toward me. "She is just as bad."

She crawled down the ladder as Bailey and I both stood at the bottom hoping and praying she didn't fall.

"I'm a grown woman," she huffed. "I don't need no god-damned babysitter." She placed her feet on the ground and tossed the broom to the side.

"All you people wanna tell me how to act, what to eat, and when," she started mumbling as she brushed off her pants. "I don't need any one standing over me making sure I don't break a hip."

She threw her hands up in the air as she turned around and began marching her way up the stairs. "And I certainly don't need no bossy ass woman telling me I can't climb a stupid ladder to swat away some bees."

The front screen door slammed behind her as she

entered the house and Bailey and I remained in the same place, staring after her.

There was a moment of silence as we both tried to register just what happened, before Bailey broke out in laughter.

"That woman is a riot, she is a hoot." Bailey held her stomach as she laughed and all I kept thinking was how I would have explained to Chase that his Nan fell off a ladder.

Bailey said her goodbyes and I chose to sit out on the front porch for a bit, allowing Nan to cool off, hopefully.

It was a nice fall day. The breeze blew through the trees and the smell of someone close cutting their grass filled the air. I loved that smell.

I leaned back in the swing, resting my head against the side and the day eventually caught up with me as I dozed off.

I was woken some time later to a gentle kiss against my lips and when I opened my eyes I came face to face with the most amazing man.

"Hi handsome." I smiled up at Chase just before he sat down at my side.

"What are you doing sleeping out here?" he asked and I'd suddenly remembered the actions that had left me a little fearful of going inside.

"Bailey and I came home after Olivia's dress fitting to find Nan up on that ladder there." I pointed toward the ladder that still remained on the grass just off the porch. "She was on top of it trying to swat away some bees."

Chase arched a brow as his gaze wandered over toward the ladder.

"She got a little pissed when Bailey asked her what on earth she was doing and she stormed off inside talking about nosy women and so on." Chase chuckled as he shook his head.

"I thought I'd stay out here for just a little while, let her calm down. I never meant to fall asleep," I assured him as I straightened up and leaned into his warm body.

He happily wrapped me in his arms as he kissed me once more.

"I'll handle Nan," he assured me. "I need to lock up the barn when I'm gone so she can't access things that I know could only get herself hurt."

There was a peace that settled over us as I curled in close to him.

"We got him," Chase whispered and I instantly sat up and turned to face him. "They arrested him last night."

"It was him?" I asked.

He nodded his head as he reached out and tucked my hair behind my ear. "He admitted that he did it." He took in a deep breath. "I sat there in that room while he confessed to hurting you and the only thing I could think about was strangling him until he had no life left in him."

The serious tone Chase took gave me the chills.

"I'm not a violent man," he said, as if I needed to hear those words.

"I know that," I assured him as I placed my outstretched hand against his cheek.

"But in that moment I could have been. I could have beat him and not even his cries would have stopped me." I could tell that acknowledgement was one he was having a hard time with.

"You're angry, hell I'm angry, but that doesn't make you a bad man. Chase," I forced him to look at me by leaning in closer. "You are a good man, and even though you say that you could do those things, I know if faced with the opportunity that goodness inside you would win."

He shook his head but I only smiled.

"You are a good man," I said once again and after a few seconds of silence he leaned in and kissed me, letting the argument fade.

Knowing that his love for me was that fierce, that he was sure he'd do whatever it took to protect me, only made me fall in love with him more.

Chase was intense.

He was mine.

And he was the father of my child, a child I knew without a doubt he would love just as fiercely.

Chapter Thirty

Chase

The fact that Keeton and his groomsmen wore dress shirts, top button open, with suit jackets and no ties was the best news I'd been given when I was asked to be part of the wedding.

I hated ties.

The girls wore cowboy boots with their dresses, making walking through the grass so much easier.

Keeton and Olivia were married on a hill, on Sawyer land. It was apparently a spot that meant something special to all of them, you could see it in their eyes.

The ceremony was emotional, for many reasons. And I felt lucky that I was a part of it.

One day I hoped Trinity and I would be sharing a day similar to this one.

She looked gorgeous, a soft pink dress that fell just above her knees, gently moving with each breeze. I think I watched her more than the actual nuptials because she was that breathtaking.

I listened to the words spoken by the preacher, the sounds of all the guests, and the Sawyers kids in the background, but all I could think of was one day she and I would be here.

And that thought didn't scare me.

But we had time; there was no need to rush.

People had children every day without marriage, but one day I would guarantee anyone who asked that Trinity would share my last name.

I sat back throughout the first part of the reception as the family exchanged hugs and tears of happiness. I watched as each of them treated Trinity as if she had been born into the Sawyer family and had never once been anything but their family.

My family was never truly close.

They were always too busy trying to outdo the other. To them it was always more about what you had in your bank account or what type of car you drove than the actual love of a real family.

It made me feel good knowing that my son or daughter would know what true love felt like, because here in Livingston they would be surrounded by it.

I smiled remembering our appointment with the doctor, just yesterday. Trinity smiled bright as the doctor placed some type of paddle looking thing against her stomach and the sound of our child's heartbeat filled the room.

We were then told that everything looked and sounded great. Come next spring we would have our child safely in our arms.

I could almost still feel that same joy.

She was only ten weeks and though she wasn't

showing yet, I looked forward to the day she did. I wanted more than anything to be able to hold her at night with my hand resting against her rounded belly.

"What are you over here smiling about?" I looked up just as Trinity stepped up next to me.

I reached out and took her hand in mine, lifting it to my lips to place a kiss along her knuckles. "I was just thinking of yesterday," I confessed. "Remembering the sounds of our baby's heartbeat and the smile on your face during that moment. It was just a happy moment."

"I guess we've never really talked about it," she said and I was instantly confused. "It was all so unplanned."

"Yeah, it was," I agreed. "But that doesn't change the fact that I love you." I leaned in and kissed the side of her mouth. "And pregnancy or not, I had every intention of keeping you real close. Now I just have more of you, because this baby is a part of me and a part of you. I'm exactly where I want to be, with the one person I can always see in my life. I want you Trin, fully, and nothing will ever change that."

She swallowed so hard I swear I heard it as her throat bobbed.

"I can't wait to meet this little person that I hope is just like their mother. Because their momma is the sweetest, kindest woman I know." Her eyes glistened with unshed tears.

"I love you, sweet girl," I whispered just before kissing her. "And I love our child so much already."

The last thing I ever wanted was for Trinity to

feel as if I regretted even one moment with her.

I already knew long before I met her that she would change my life. Had I known it would be to this extent? No. But never would I ever change a thing that had happened between her and me.

"Dance with me," Trinity said.

As if I could deny her.

I hooked my arm around her waist and pulled her body to mine. "I'd love too."

I couldn't promise I wouldn't be terrible at it, or that I wouldn't step on her toes more than once, but I'd try. Because she wanted me to. I'd do anything for her.

I allowed her to lead me toward the area where every other person had gathered to dance. And she turned to face me, wearing that smile I loved so much, I stepped up close and took her in my arms.

She felt right in my arms. It was like she had always been there, as if that very spot was created just for her.

"I love you, Chase," she whispered.

I looked over toward my Nan, who at that moment was watching the two of us close and she smiled at me.

She hadn't said as much, but I knew that she had also fallen in love with Trinity.

She offered me a nod of her head and I squeezed Trinity just a little tighter.

"I love you too, baby," I whispered in return. "More than I'll ever be able to express. You're my world, sweetheart."

I heard her sigh and I knew just what she was feeling because right then, everything felt like it was exactly as it should be.

Chapter Thirty- One

Trinity

I woke in tears for the third time in three weeks. The dreams felt so real. The pain and agony that made my chest ache so severely.

I'd heard and read of the dreams that were sometimes brought on during pregnancy, but nothing ever prepared me for the actual experiences of those dreams.

And they were all the same.

I rested my hands over my slightly swollen belly that in just the last couple of weeks seemed to make an appearance.

The physical presence of my tiny baby bump gave me the reassurance that my dreams were just that, dreams.

I wasn't still trapped in the life I once led with an evil man. I had the unconditional love of an amazing man who stood by my side and accepted me, flaws and all.

Once I had calmed my racing heart I moved from

the bed and down the hall toward the kitchen. It was just barely after 7:00 and usually by now I could smell some sorta something cooking in the kitchen.

Only this morning everything was so quiet. No banging of pans or fresh coffee brewing. It was eerily quiet.

Chase had gone into the station early to finish up some paperwork he didn't do last night. And Nan was usually up and moving by now, but there was nothing.

I continued through the kitchen and toward Nan's room only to find her door was still shut.

I paused for a moment as I pressed my ear to the door and listened for any signs that she may be moving around.

But again there was nothing.

My stomach tensed, giving me that feeling one gets when they know something is wrong.

I tapped on the door.

"Nan," I said, pausing for her response that never came.

My stomach only tensed more.

"Nan, are you there?" I asked once again as I placed my hand on the knob and began to turn.

My heart immediately began to race as I looked into the darkened room and found Nan lying on the floor near her bed, with her eyes closed.

I rushed forward and knelt by her side. "Nan, please." I practically begged her to say something, to do anything. I just wanted to see those irritated eyes and hear her complain about me being too protective. I wanted her to yell and tell me that if she wanted to lie on her damn floor that was her choice not mine.

But nothing came.

I felt for a pulse and was immediately relieved to find she did have one. Rapid, but it was there.

I tried to remain calm as I went in search of a phone. Nan was still one of those old school ladies who believed in house phones versus a cell phone. There in the hallway sat a cordless phone on the charging base.

My hands shook as I dialed 911 and began moving back toward Nan, who still lay in the same place.

"911, what's your emergency?" the young woman asked as she answered the call.

"I need an ambulance at 1842 Furrow Lane." My voice shook just as much as my hands.

"Okay ma'am, can you talk to me and tell me what's going on?" she asked.

"Please send them now," I practically begged.

"They're on their way, but as they are I would like to get some further information for them. I can dispatch the nature of the emergency through to the EMTs if you'll just tell me a little about what's going on." She was so calm and that seemed to help because on the inside I was slowly falling apart.

Nan meant so much to Chase, and she had also begun to mean so much to me. The thought of something happening to her devastated me. I couldn't imagine what this would do to Chase.

"My grandmother," I said as I again took her hand in mine. "I don't know what's wrong; I just found her crumpled on the floor, and she's breathing but unresponsive to my voice."

"Does she have any previous health concerns that we need to know about?" she asked.

I tried to remember everything Chase had told me about Nan. The medication she took, the recent visits to her doctor.

"Liver disease, Rheumatoid Arthritis," I said in a rush. "And, um…" God, what couldn't I remember? I squeezed my eyes shut tightly and recalled a conversation one morning over breakfast when Chase was harping on his grandmother about her health.

"And Coronary Artery Disease." It was a joke between Nan and Chase because when he got all worked up, she would say, "Stop having a damn coronary, boy." It only pissed him off more that she was making light of her health.

"Okay, the ambulance is only a few minutes away, but we've relayed all the information you provided to them. They are well aware of the patient." She talked to me, continuing to ask questions about her current condition.

She had me check her pulse and continue to talk to her, trying to gain some sense of response.

Once I let the paramedics inside, I stepped back and watched as they took over. With each passing moment I only managed to grow more fearful.

Chapter Thirty-Two

Chase

I sat in the passenger seat of the squad car, laughing at the look on Noah's face. "She tried man, she did. But every single time she tried to say sick, she said dick." His face was red and his eyes shined as he laughed through the words he spoke.

"Do you know how hard it was to keep a straight face while my daughter is standing in front of me telling me over and over that she got dick three times that day?" His eyes widened as he tried to fight his smile.

"I wanted to be pissed at the thought but hell, she looked so cute holding her blanket close to her face, looking up at me with those big brown eyes of hers." He shook his head. "Alena stood a few feet away hiding her smile in a damn dishtowel she held to her mouth."

"Had Nora been fifteen and was saying the same thing, I'd been out the door carrying my shot gun looking for the little fucker that got anywhere near my daughter," he said with a serious tone.

Apparently little Nora had a speech impediment and the sweet girl was always stumping her parents every time she got carried away with an explanation. But this one right here topped all the other stories I had heard.

Just then my cell phone began to ring and I reached into my pocket to retrieve it.

It was a number I didn't recognize.

"Yeah," I said as I placed the phone to my ear.

"Chase, is that you?" a woman asked.

"Yeah this is Chase," I assured her.

"It's Tammy," she clarified and I instantly wondered why Tammy Sawyer would be calling me. Unless something was wrong with Trinity.

My heart sank.

"Is Trinity okay?" I sat forward in the seat and gripped the dashboard.

"Trinity is fine, but I stopped by the house about fifteen minutes ago and they were loading your grandmother into an ambulance." My chest ached as she continued. "Trinity found her this morning in her bedroom and she wasn't responding to her, so she called 911."

"Trin is in the ambulance with her and I'm following behind. She asked me to call you because in the mass confusion of the moment she couldn't find her phone to call you herself." I was thankful that she was by Nan's side.

"I'm on my way," I said as I hit "end" and looked toward Noah.

"I need you to take me to the hospital," I said, still feeling my heart race with all the possibilities.

Noah just nodded his head, turned the key in the ignition, and put the car in drive. We had been enjoying a coffee that we'd picked up at Amber's café just moments ago. Laughing and joking about the things little Nora said that confused her parents, but now that happy carefree time was over.

I felt a strong sense of loss.

Over the last year and a half I had lived side by side with a woman who, on most days, drove me nuts. She was complicated, insane, and the biggest god-damn headache, but I couldn't imagine my life without her. Besides all those things, she had also been my rock. She had been my best friend and one of my biggest supporters.

A life without Nan was one I had refrained from thinking about. I wasn't ready for that world. I wasn't sure I ever would be.

***

As I rounded the corner that led to the waiting area, I found Trinity pacing the hall. Her head was hung as she looked at the floor. Her hands were in front of her as she continued to worryingly twist them over and over.

She had not yet noticed me moving toward her. But just as I stepped up to her side she looked in my direction, and it was then that I noticed her red-rimmed eyes.

She and Nan had grown close. Nan had accepted this beautiful girl as part of our little family too and she loved her just as I did.

Nan was not the type who showed her emotions

often, but I could see the love in her eyes when she watched Trinity.

This day was hard on my girl too.

Without hesitation I wrapped her in my arms and held her close as I rocked her from side to side. Neither of us spoke because at that point there was no news. It was the waiting game.

The one where family is left in the dark, with the worst possible feelings and the medical staff doing everything they could to ensure the best possible outcome.

That game sucked.

"I shouldn't have hit snooze on the alarm clock," Trinity said with her face buried against my chest. "I should have gotten up and I would…"

"No," I whispered as I pushed her back away from me and forced her to look at me. "This is not your fault. It's no one's fault."

"But if I…" she began, but I cut her off before she could finish.

"I didn't check on her either," I said, and she looked up at me as tears filled her eyes once again. "Nan is stubborn, sweet girl; we've been chastised to many times for hovering. No, this is not anyone's fault."

Even though on the inside I felt slightly responsible, I refused to let Trinity continue to feel even the slightest amount of blame.

I also didn't want her to get too overwhelmed or upset because I assumed that wasn't great for her or the baby. "Why don't we go sit down?" I asked but didn't wait for her response. Instead I started moving toward the waiting area, with my arm around her waist.

"Do you need anything to drink? Eat?" I asked as I motioned toward the chairs in front of us.

She offered me a gentle smile and shook her head as she sat down, not letting go of my hand. I lowered myself to the chair beside her and without hesitation moved my hand from hers to place my arm over her shoulder.

I just wanted to feel her close.

I had that sense of déjà vu from the night I'd been here not that long ago. Only on that night I was waiting for news of Trinity's condition instead.

Chapter Thirty-Three

Trinity

"How is she?" Ryan asked as he sat down on the bar stool next to me. I'd stopped off at the bakery to grab some breakfast for Chase and me before heading back to the hospital.

"Feisty," I said with a smile.

"That's good, right?" he asked as he winked at Amber when she passed him his morning coffee.

"Yeah, it's good," I laughed. "Unless you're one of the nurses trying to take care of her or the doctor who's offering direction."

Winnie Willard was a force to be reckoned with. She had a fire in her that I didn't think would ever burn out. She would be on her death bed letting everyone around her have it. At least until she took her very last breath.

"Well, I'm real glad she's okay." Ryan bumped my shoulder with his before he stood and leaned over to give Amber a kiss.

"Chase said to tell you he'll be back at the

station tomorrow," I offered as he stepped back from the counter.

"You tell Chase that I said to take care of Nan, and when she's home safe and all is well, then he can come back to the station." Ryan was a good man. Family was number one, always, with the Sawyers.

"Thanks," I said, and he leaned in to offer a brotherly kiss to my temple.

"You got it," he said just before turning around and heading to the patrol car idling along the curb.

"I threw in a few extra mini apple pie wraps because I know Chase loves those." Amber sat a pink box in front of me. She had all the guys in our family spoiled and now she'd added Chase to that mix. I swore she could make a dishrag taste good with just a few ingredients. The woman was a genius.

"Thank you," I told her as I got up and grabbed the box of yummy goodness.

"Of course. I'm so glad that Winnie is feeling better. She gave us all a scare with that stubborn heart of hers, but I gotta ask." She tilted her head to the side and gave me a serious look. "How are you feeling?"

I had been feeling fine so her concern was a little unexpected.

"I just know that so much has gone on. From the moment we were all aware of your pregnancy I just worried that none of us have truly taken the time to tell you how happy we are for you." Amber was always so sweet and concerned for everyone around her.

"I'm real good," I assured her.

"You do know if you need anything at any time, Ryan and I are here for you, no matter what."

I did know that. Because it was just who they were. They had three little boys who were a handful. Crazy little devils full of so much energy one wished they could bottle it up and use it for themselves. But never, not once, did Ryan and Amber ever turn anyone in need away.

"I know," I said with a smile. "And don't worry about me, everything is good, I promise."

And it was.

I was rounding my fourth month, and feeling amazing. I was starting to show and no longer just looked like I was packing on weight from eating too many sweets. My tiny belly was proof enough that I had a little person to thank for my excess weight.

Nan was getting better every day, even though for a while there we were terrified that we might have to get used to that big ole house without her there to liven the place up.

Chase seemed less stressed, which always made me feel better too.

Things were good.

***

"What the hell are y'all doing here anyway?" I could hear his booming voice before I even entered the room. "You never gave a shit before. Hell, where the hell have you people been for the last year?"

I paused outside Nan's room wondering if I

should enter.

Rarely did I witness Chase in a hostile state. At this moment it was evident that whatever was going on, he was pissed about it.

"Listen, boy, this has nothing to do with you." A woman spoke and there was something about her condescending tone toward Chase that made me feel irritated. "That is my mother."

And in that moment I understood just why Chase was angry.

His mother was there. Inside that room. A daughter who had turned her back on her own mother. A woman who until now didn't give a shit about Nan's health or her wellbeing. The only thing she did care about was whether she got an inheritance she felt she was entitled to.

"Nothing to do with me?" Chase said with a laugh that gave me the chills. "This has everything to do with me." His voice remained calm but anyone who truly knew him would understand he was barely hanging onto his patience. "I've taken care of her every day for almost two years. I never once asked for anything in return because I didn't expect anything. That is what you call love, Mother. A word you are not accustomed too."

"How dare you talk to your mother like that?" Another man's voice broke through all the anger-fueled words and I moved without any further hesitation.

I don't know what it was in that moment that made me feel bold, but I knew that I didn't like the tone either one of them carried when speaking with Chase.

I pushed open the door and all eyes turned to me. Nan's bed was empty and that explained why these people were openly arguing with Chase.

"Where's Nan?" I asked, forgetting all about the two idiots who looked at me like I stumbled into the wrong room by mistake.

Chase pushed past his father and walked toward me. "They took her for an EKG. She'll be back soon." He placed his hands on my hips and shot a look back over his shoulder where both his mother and father continued to stare at me like I was some filthy creature.

I instantly hated them and vowed to keep them far away from my child. They were obviously poison.

"Maybe you should head back home for a bit," he said as he turned to face me once again. I shook my head to argue and I watched as he fought not to smile. "I think Nan is rubbing off on my girl; you never used to be so stubborn."

"Who is this?" hissed his mother.

"Not that it's any business of yours," Chase said in return, with just as much venom as she was spewing. "This is Trinity."

I didn't let it offend me that he offered her very few details about me. I knew it was more because she didn't deserve to know versus being ashamed of me.

"This doesn't concern her." His father was the one who spoke that time. The anger in Chase quickly returned.

"This concerns her as much as me. This woman has been there for Nan more than you ever have."

He practically growled the words.

I soothingly rubbed his arm, trying to gain his attention, but he continued to stare down his father.

"Looks like she found a meal ticket to support her," Chase's mother said with a sneer. "Please tell me you're not responsible for her current condition."

Chase moved faster than I could stop him. He stepped up to face both of his parents and squared his shoulders. "I used to think the two of you hung the damn moon. My whole life I wanted to be just like my father, and one day find a woman to care for my children the way my own mother cared for me. Because in my eyes you two were the most caring and loving people." He laughed sarcastically. "But then as I grew older I saw the real people behind the façade. Heartless, greedy people, who cared for no one but themselves."

I wanted to reach out and comfort him because a life like he had just described was no kind of life to live. I had not come from a magical world of peace and love, but knowing that this loving man came from these people before me broke my heart.

"I won't give either of you the satisfaction of ruining anything for me because even the poison you reek of couldn't taint what I share with Trinity. She's nothing like you. She's sweet, kind, and so full of love. She is the person who has shown me what true honest love feels like. And yes, she is carrying my child." His mother wrinkled her nose in disgust. "My child, who I can assure you neither of you will know. The hate you carry will never touch my child."

Chapter Thirty-Four

Chase

I knew they were heartless. I knew they were hateful.

But I think somewhere down deep I had held out for the possibility that somewhere within them they still held some piece of humanity left.

But their actions today proved me wrong.

They weren't the parents I thought they were when I was growing up.

They were everything I didn't want to be.

Had I remained in that hospital room with them a moment longer I'm sure I would have lost it. But Trinity being the woman she was knew I needed air.

She took my hand in hers and without even a backward glance, led me out of the room and down the hall.

The moment we stepped outside she turned to face me, rose up on the tip of her toes, and took my face in her hands.

"You are nothing like them," she whispered just

before pressing her lips to mine. "You're so gentle and caring and you do that because you are an amazing man, not out of obligation."

I continued to stare back at her as she watched me, and held my face. "I'm sorry you have to deal with the hatred they bring, but you're stronger than they are. Please don't let them get to you because that is exactly what people like them strive for. They will kick you when you're down and be smug when you fail."

I knew she was right. But the anger I felt toward them was consuming. They deserted Nan. They left her here alone when she refused to sign everything she owned over to them. They wanted to put her in a home, for Christ's sake.

I couldn't imagine that woman in a nursing home.

She would rain fire on the place.

"Nothing they say or do can ever change the man you are," Trinity continued. "A man I love with all my heart, and Nan does too. They don't matter; their words mean nothing."

I stared back at her as I allowed what she said to really sink in.

She was right.

I knew she was right.

I just got so lost in the anger I had for them that I let their words eat away at me.

"Have I told you lately how amazing you are?" I asked as she cocked her head in the cute quirky way she did when I gave her a compliment. "Because you are, and the way you calm me, the way you give me a sense of clarity even in my weakest of times, just confirms how perfect you are."

"I'm not perfect, Chase," she whispered in return and it was my turn to take her face in my hands.

"You're perfect for me," I whispered as I tilted my head toward hers and pressed my lips against hers. "I love you, sweet girl, so damn much."

After Trinity calmed me I had no intention of revisiting the hell that accompanied my parents. So I made a very calm suggestion to the both of them that they hit the road before I had them removed.

The look on their faces when I spoke those words gave me tremendous gratification. I knew we weren't rid of them yet. That would have been entirely too easy and nothing was ever easy with them.

Instead I enjoyed the remaining part of the day with Nan. And my evening with the most beautiful woman wrapped in my arms.

It was exactly how I imagined spending the remainder of my days. And soon we'd have a little piece of us here to share it with too.

***

Nan had been home for less than an hour when the hell started.

The assholes didn't even allow the engine in my truck to cool before they pulled in the drive in their expensive rental.

But Nan was ready for a fight, I could see it in her eyes. She had that smug take no shit look on her face.

The minute my parents walked in the front door,

she gave them no time to start.

"Well, if it isn't my loving and devoted family, who has been by my side through every hardship of the last two years of my life." She plastered on the fakest of smiles and I tried not to laugh.

Poor Trinity looked like she had no idea what she should do. Run and hide, or just grab a bowl of popcorn and pull up a chair.

"Love the sarcasm, Mother." My mother said the word with pure disgust.

I honestly had no idea why it was that both of my parents had such disrespect toward Nan. They had once been close. I remember growing up around both my grandparents and seeing my parents laugh and share holidays here at the farm.

Could it all really fall apart over money? And property?

Did family mean that little to my parents?

But I remained silent.

Because this fight was Nan's.

A fight I knew she was more than willing to take control of and conquer. She'd been gearing up for this for close to two years.

I would remain silent unless provoked.

"Now what are you talking about, my dear daughter?" Again, full sarcasm.

Did I mention how much I adore my grandmother and her ability to lay the shit on thick?

"You know why we're here." My father broke into the line of the stare down my mother and Nan were currently having.

"No, my dear son-in-law, I don't, but something tells me you're about to tell me. And I'm all giddy inside." Nan faked a shiver and I couldn't have held back the laughter that time even if I wanted too.

I think I even heard a giggle escape Trinity that time.

"After your recent health concern, we think it is best that we move you into Tall Oaks where you'll be watched over at all times." My mother tried to play the concern card. "We worry that you'll have an instance again where you need help yet no one will be there to offer it."

Nan didn't respond, she only watched them, waiting. It was concerning that she wasn't arguing, but I continued to remain silent.

"We worry about you," my mother added.

Was she fucking serious?

"Since when?" I hadn't spoken until then but I couldn't stop myself. "Because not once over the last year have you called or stopped in to see how she was. You don't care."

"Boy," Nan said in a warning tone and I hung my head like a scolded child.

Her fight. I had to remember that.

"The only thing you two are worried about is what you feel you're entitled to." And here came the good stuff, I thought. "But now it is time for me to talk."

I wanted to rub my hands together like you do when excitement hits just before a really big moment.

"When I do kick the bucket and all you damn fools come running thinking you're about to rake in the Willard dough, you'll all still come up empty-handed." Nan smiled bright and even though I knew her words were not strictly directed toward me, I didn't feel an ounce of disappointment knowing I wouldn't get a penny.

It was never about the money.

"Everything I have," Nan continued, "and all I have ever had, goes to that boy right there."

She didn't even look at me, but she pointed.

"Because he is the only real family I've had. He and that girl of his never once turned their backs on me. They are here for me because they want to be, because they care. Not for the money or the property. They've never expected a damn thing in return."

Both my parents looked completely shocked and angry.

"So keep waiting." She shrugged. "But you'll be waiting a long damn time."

Neither of my parents spoke but I did.

"Nan," I whispered hoarsely. I'd never expected to be left anything; it was never the reason behind being here for her.

But she refused to let me argue.

"Chase, you are the only one in my family who stepped forward when I needed help. You are selfless and nothing would make me happier than leaving everything your grandfather worked so hard for to you."

And just like that Nan settled it.

Trinity remained silent and we all watched as my parents angrily left the house knowing that their so-called concern was not going to get them the only thing they truly came to Livingston for.

Chapter Thirty-Five

Trinity

"Just watch him," Nan whispered as she quietly eyed Chase as he moved around gathering his coffee in his mug.

He was fully dressed in uniform and ready to head off to work, yet Nan, I could tell, had a touch of the ornery bug this morning.

The two of them were something else.

"Hey boy," she said as she slightly leaned back in the chair and placed her hands on the table top casually.

Chase looked back over his shoulder, waiting for her to continue.

"Grab my teeth," she said, doing her best to hold back her smile. This was an ongoing thing with these two. Chase hated it.

I loved the torment Nan gave him just because she knew how much it got under his skin.

It was his fault, really; he showed his weakness. And with a person like Nan, you never showed weakness.

The look on his face was one of horror. He looked over toward the sink and we could tell he had zoned in on the offensive container that held her teeth just inside.

His nose wrinkled and it was taking everything I had not to laugh at his expression.

"They ain't no bomb, boy," she added, still playing it all out very impressively. "Just snatch 'em up and bring 'em over." She waved her hand in the air, motioning for him to get a move on.

His eyes shifted toward me for help but these days, it had gotten harder and harder for me to get up once I sat down.

Over the last few months I felt like I'd tripled in size.

I was just shy of eight months, living in a house with the two feistiest people I knew and loving every moment of it. I still worked at Sassy Ladies, but only part time because Chase insisted.

But on mornings like this that started off with Nan teasing Chase and me getting to see him squirm, it made me realize how lucky I was to have found them both.

Chase was still debating on how he could get out of touching his Nan's teeth when the back door came open and in walked Olivia.

"Morning all," she said as she walked in and offered Chase a little push on his shoulder before walking toward Nan and me.

I looked back over at Chase and in that moment it was as if I could almost hear what he was thinking. He had that crazy gleam in his eyes as he screwed the lid onto his traveling mug and then his gaze settled on me.

He mouthed "I love you" just before he grabbed his keys and moved quickly toward the door. "Hey Liv, Nan needs her teeth," he hollered out. "They're by the sink in the blue container. Have a good day, ladies."

He had casually dodged that bullet and Olivia was in the line of fire.

And as if it wasn't funny enough to see Chase disgustingly horrified by Nan's teeth, Olivia managed to make it even funnier.

She walked over toward the sink, looked down in the container and shivered. "Eww, is that food floating in there?" she whined, and gagged for dramatic effect.

The sound of Nan's laughter followed by even more gagging on Olivia's part did me in and I could no longer hold back my own laughter.

"Have I mentioned lately how much I love this life?" Nan said in the midst of all her laughter and I had to agree. Life was good.

***

"Are these maternity clothes?" I asked in awe as I held up the most adorable top I've ever seen.

Alena stepped up to my side and ran her hand over the material. "Yes, I figured with all the pregnancy going around I should start carrying something fashionable."

It took a moment to register her words before I gave her an odd look. As far as I knew I was the only one pregnant.

Alena bit her lip and softly nodded her head and I couldn't contain my excitement. "Are you?" I couldn't even finish my sentence before she started nodding her head.

"Oh my God," I squealed just as the bell above the door chimed and in walked Noah and Chase.

"You tell her?" Noah asked.

"Tell her what?" It was Chase's turn to ask.

"Alena's pregnant," I said in a rush because damn it, I wanted to tell someone and Chase was *my someone.*

"Congratulations man, but I've been with you today for more than four hours and you couldn't share the news?" Chase turned to look at Noah.

"How the hell you expect me to say shit when all you talk about is Trinity?" Noah replied. "You're like a damn girl, gabbing and aww-ing. A guy can't get a word in edgewise with you in the room."

I could tell Noah was just being a Sawyer, dealing shit and making Chase squirm. Those men loved that Chase cared for me so much. It made them happy knowing I had a man who would do anything and give his all to keep me safe. Just as he had with Charlie.

Chase went to every court date, every single questioning that he could. He stood back quietly observing and giving his opinion only when he was allowed. He made it his goal to make sure Charlie got what he deserved.

And even though he said he'd have killed him if given the opportunity, I knew different. Because throughout all the hatred and anger, Chase still did what he could to make sure Charlie got the help he needed to get clean. He wanted the reassurance of knowing that on the inside, behind the bars that would house Charlie for three years, that he'd learn the fundamentals to change his world. He was now seeing a counselor and even Charlie's father was going to see him each Saturday as they tried to rebuild their relationship.

I never said much about all the things Chase worked on during that time, because in a way I still believed he felt as if he shouldn't have cared. But he was wrong. Him setting aside his anger and frustration over the things Charlie had done to me just showed me what kind of man he truly was. It was just confirmation that Chase Douglas was in fact the sweetest, kindest man.

A man I would spend the rest of my life loving.

Epilogue

Chase

"Just one more push, Trinity." The nurse coached her as I watched in amazement. "You got it."

The moment the loud cries filled the room I felt my body turn to what I would refer to as putty. I was in awe of the woman before me. She was a god-damn super hero.

Trinity closed her eyes as her body relaxed back against the bed.

Those angry cries of our child continued as the nurses moved around the room.

I leaned over the woman who had in a matter of seconds given me the greatest gift anyone could ever give another person and pressed my lips to her forehead. "I know I've said it before," I whispered, "but you are truly amazing."

"Would you like to meet your son?"

I turned quickly to find a nurse standing at my side, holding my son wrapped securely in a blue blanket.

I couldn't speak, because the emotions running through me were overwhelming. Instead I nodded my head as she moved my son from her arms to mine.

He was so tiny, so perfect.

He made these soft little snorting sounds as he moved his head around before finding a comfortable position.

My vision blurred as tears pooled in my eyes and I did nothing to stop them.

I was a father.

And in that moment, I just knew.

It wasn't the most romantic of places. And it probably wasn't what Trinity had envisioned, but I didn't care.

I looked over at her as she smiled up at me, watching me hold our son and I knew what I wanted. I knew what I couldn't wait even one more seconds to say.

"Marry me," I whispered and that smile that was covering her lips shifted to shock for just a moment before her smile returned. "I want to spend the rest of my life with you, sharing moments like these."

"Yes," she replied and I leaned in to press my lips to hers.

There we were in the delivery room, with the doctor and nurses staring back at us and I'd just proposed. It had been something I'd known for months I wanted, yet I held off thinking there was no need to rush. Only now I wanted to call the preacher that married Olivia and Keeton and bring him here.

I wanted Trinity to share my last name. The same last name our son would have, and all our children that followed.

"I want more kids," I mumbled against her lips and she laughed. "A house full."

"Slow down there, Superman," she said. "Let me get used to the idea of having one before you go planting another."

Trinity

I stood next to Liam's crib as I watched him sleep. He was the most happy, peaceful baby. It'd been three weeks since we brought him home and each day I fell in love with him all over again.

He looked just like his daddy and I knew one day he would for sure break some hearts of his own.

Strong arms circled my waist as Chase stepped up behind me. "What are you doing?" he whispered near my ear.

"Just watching him sleep," I confessed.

"I do that too," Chase replied and I smiled because I already knew that. I had woken up so many times throughout the night to find the bed empty at my side. After going to search for him, I'd find that he was in the nursery, just watching our son sleep.

"It's still so hard to believe that he's ours," Chase added and I couldn't have agreed more. "And soon he'll have brothers and sisters to keep him fully entertained."

I could sense his smile.

"You still living that fantasy, Mr. Douglas?" I

said in return, wearing my own smile.

"Can't blame me really," he said, swaying from side to side, gently moving our bodies as one. "We make gorgeous kids. I mean really, look at him and tell me you don't want ten more like him."

"Ten?" I said, a little horrified by the number.

"Okay, five," Chase corrected, but I still didn't feel great about that number either.

"How about two?" I looked back over my shoulder, waiting for him to assure me I would not be barefoot and pregnant with little Douglas children for the next five to eight years of my life.

"Three," he whispered, "but I will be secretly aiming for five."

"You're hopeless," I said just before he kissed me.

"But you love me," he whispered against my lips and I couldn't argue. I did love him, hopelessly and unconditionally.

Chase Douglas, I believed, was the man I was meant to spend forever with. All the ugly in my life had led me to this point, right here.

So if living in hell was what I had to do in order to find this man, then I would gladly suffer it over again if it meant I had this in the end.

Because this right here was what I imagined perfect to be.

A Year Later

Amber

"Rogan," I marched down the hall toward the

living room with determination. There in the center of the floor sat all three of my boys, staring back at me as if I'd lost my mind. And maybe I had, but that is what three boys spawned from a Sawyer man will do to any woman.

In my hand I held yet another one of my expensive blouses from Sassy Ladies, covered in mud.

I knew exactly who the culprit was.

Rogan Larson Sawyer.

My eyes were focused on him as he looked up at me giving his best innocent look. Those big puppy dog eyes he, as well as Rory, inherited straight from their daddy.

On most days those sweet eyes would get them out of the worst possible situations. But not today.

"What have I told you about using my shirts to clean off your dump trucks after you run them through the mud?" He continued to stare up at me.

And after a moment he hung his head and whispered his apology. "I sorry, momma."

Did I mention the other way these three boys played me like a fiddle?

Those sad little voices, as they hung their heads as if disappointed in themselves. I wasn't a pushover, I knew damn well they had figured out just how to play their mom. And I wasn't the only one. Not many withstood the little boy charm my mini Ryans held.

It was a gift.

A gift that was abused.

"How is Mommy supposed to look pretty if you keep on ruining my pretty things?" I asked as I sat down on the floor in front of all three of them and reached out to tip Rogan's chin upward.

"Because you look pretty in everything you wear, darlin'," Ryan said, causing us all to turn around toward the direction he came from.

There in the doorway stood the most handsome man in Livingston. He still after all this time made my heart race and my knees go weak.

Ryder wasted no time before he scrambled from the floor and sprinted across the living room to jump into Ryan's arms. He was a daddy's boy through and through, even though he was the spitting image of me.

"Isn't momma the prettiest lady around?" he asked Ryder as he tickled his stomach.

"Yesh," my handsome little man agreed and the twins moved toward me, throwing their arms round my neck and practically tackling me to the floor.

I was surrounded by boys, and I knew that years from now I would be begging for a break from all the testosterone. But for now I couldn't get enough. Ryan's happiness, and the love of my boys, meant the world to me. Olivia and I were as close as two could get and I loved the time we shared together.

Every day I sent up a thanks to the woman I never met but felt like I knew so well. Because I knew she was the one who showed Ryan how to love the way he does.

Tammy raised him to be a gentleman. She raised him to treat a woman like a lady. But I believed it was Claire who showed Ryan what it meant to truly love someone with your whole heart.

And forever would I be thankful for that gift she

gave him.

My heart couldn't love him more than I already did. Because he was, and would forever be, my everything.

Ryan

"Where ya heading?" Chase asked as I climbed up in my truck outside of the station.

"Heading home to pick up my wife for a weekend away," I said as I placed the key in the ignition and turned. "Boys are with Liv, and the bags are packed."

"Nice," he said with a nod of his head.

He looked exhausted as he stared off into the distance, his own keys in his hand.

"Is everything okay?" I asked and he looked back at me as if I pulled him out of some deep thought.

He blew out an exasperated breath and ran his hands through his hair. "Just stalling, I guess," he confessed.

I wanted to laugh. In a way I already knew what the guy was going through, but it was his own damn fault.

"She is pissed off all the time," he mumbled and I remained silent, letting him ramble. "She wants chocolate ice cream, I go in search of chocolate, but the time I get back she's pissed because she wants strawberry instead. I can't win."

He looked me straight in the eyes and I swear his expression was one of desperation. "It wasn't like this before. With Liam she was so sweet. But I swear the damn devil has possessed my wife and she might kill me in my sleep one night."

It was then I laughed.

"What the hell is so funny?" he asked. "I sleep with one eye open and one leg hanging off the bed touching the floor at my side. This way if I have to move fast I feel I'm one step closer."

He didn't smile. There was absolutely no humor in his words.

"Weren't you the one that said you wanted five kids?" I asked.

"I changed my mind. After this one, we're done. I want Trinity back." Again, complete seriousness.

Poor guy looked lost.

And it was the best damn thing to witness.

Within four months of having Liam, Trinity was pregnant again. And this time she was cranky as hell. Everyone noticed it, but she directed all that aggravation toward the man she said was to blame.

And the rest of us loved to witness his hell.

I remember Amber's pregnancy with Ryder. She cried all the time, she'd be exhausted one minute, and attacking me the next.

Those times were my favorite.

I smiled remembering the times I'd just let her take control. My little wildcat.

"You're still smiling," Chase complained.

If he only knew the thoughts running through my mind had absolutely nothing to do with him.

"Go home, Chase," I told him and he looked as if he wanted to argue.

"Stop at the store and pick up every flavor of ice cream they got," I told him. "Tell her she's beautiful and rub her feet."

"I do that already," he whined. "I tell her she's beautiful, and no other woman has ever looked as amazing as her. I tell her I love her and that she is my world, but she is like the exorcist."

"Well it's your job to take it. Let her growl and complain and just take it," I told him. "Because at the end of the day you just need to remember one thing."

He looked at me like I was about to give him the best piece of advice. I almost felt bad about the fact that I had nothing reassuring to say.

"What?" he asked and I cracked a smile, almost talking myself out of taking the chance at being an asshole. Then I thought about the fact that had the roles been reversed he would have jumped at the chance.

"You are to blame for the state she is in." He narrowed his eyes at me. "And the rest of us guys are loving that it's you and not us being tortured."

"You're an asshole," he mumbled as he turned around and walked off toward his truck.

I laughed the entire drive home.

Bailey

"Belle, do not put makeup on your brother." I stood in the hallway holding Billy on my hip as I noted the damage.

"Is that my eyeliner?" I hollered when I noticed the black line that trailed along his eyes just an inch above his eyelashes.

Then I leaned in a little closer and sniffed.

"And my Dolce and Gabbana!" Oh, now it was on.

Billy giggled as I gripped him tighter and marched toward Belle's room. As I entered the room I froze and blinked a few times trying to register what I was seeing.

"Annabelle Rose Sawyer," I said, trying so hard to control my irritation. "Is that my wedding dress?"

"Yeah, Mommy." She looked up at me with excitement and pure joy. "Don't I look beautiful? Just like you in your pictures."

Her tiny little body was lost in a sea of silk and sequins. And she looked absolutely ridiculous with bright red lipstick and blue eyeshadow that went all the way up to her eyebrow.

But I couldn't be mad.

God forbid she had turned my son into her best version of a drag queen, and had Jackson walked in then, he would have whisked his son off to root in the mud while talking of trucks and fish.

He refused to allow Billy to even pick up a doll without replacing it with something dirty and boyish.

Billy wiggled in my arms, causing me to lower him to the floor before he managed to get free on his own.

Within seconds my little man had managed to get beneath the dress with his sister and now both of them were squeezed in the bodice and smiling brightly up at me.

It was a sight I was sure I would never forget.

At the sound of the front door, Billy's eyes grew wide as he scrambled to break free from the hold my custom made dress had on him and before I could stop him he shot past me like a bullet in search of his daddy.

I stood frozen, covering my mouth to hide the laughter that was threatening to spill out of me. I waited for the reaction I knew was coming.

"Bailey," Jackson practically growled from the other room and I scrambled inside my daughter's room and hid behind the mini bride. Her cuteness was bound to protect me right?

When Jackson appeared in the doorway holding Billy in his arms, I smiled up at him alongside my daughter.

"Why in the you-know-what is my son wearing perfume and makeup?" He arched a brow looking displeased.

I looked at Belle, she looked at me, and before she could play the daughter girl card, I did what I had to do.

I ratted out my daughter.

"She did it," I said, pointing toward Annabelle, and she turned her head back to her father and smiled up at him with red lipstick smeared all across her front teeth.

And what did my big, burly, and too sexy for his own good husband do?

He looked back at her and winked.

"Well, sweetheart, I think you should be a makeup artist one day because he looks marvelous."

Belle giggled, Billy squared his tiny little shoulders, puffed out his chest and his toothless grin matched hers.

And I sat there, wondering what in the hell just

happened.

My daughter was magical, that was the only explanation. She had some kind of calming power that took an intense moment and made everything all right.

Jackson

I could hear Bailey's shoes scuffing along the gravel as she walked around the side of the barn in search of me.

With the kids and the ranch, we rarely had the time we used to have to sneak off and get a little alone time. But that was about to be rectified.

"Jackson," she hollered in search of me. Just as she stepped through the doorway, and without a second more of hesitation, I hooked her around the waist and pulled her body flush against mine.

She squealed in surprise as I covered her mouth with mine and pressed her against the wall, using my hips to pin her.

I swallowed her moan as I pressed my hardness against her. It had been too many nights since I'd gotten lost in her warmth and I was a starving man.

"Jackson," she whimpered as my greedy girl practically climbed me like a tree and hooked her legs around my waist. "We can't do this," she protested, but her body was telling me something else.

I gripped her hips tight as I pushed against her harder. "I think we can," I moaned when she shifted against me in return. "In fact, I know we can. And we can do it very," I nipped at her neck, "very well."

"The kids…" she tried to protest but I refused to let her.

"The kids are fine. Noah and Ryan are inside. Ma has them fully entertained, so can you just let me have what I want." I smiled when she moaned as I pushed at her once again. "And what I already know you want too."

"Yes," she sighed. "Please, yes."

And there was the girl I'd fallen in love with. My needy, do it anywhere anytime girl.

I slid my palms around to squeeze her ass as I held her up and moved her toward the counter lining the makeshift office I used to conduct any meeting regarding horse training.

The moment I lowered her she started working her shorts loose in a hurry. I chuckled at the shift in her mood. Only moments ago she was trying to find reasons why we shouldn't, but now she couldn't get her clothes off fast enough.

I watched in awe as she unhooked her legs from my waist and shimmied her hips from side to side as she removed her shorts and panties in one swift move.

I wanted to make some dirty comment regarding her eager behavior but I didn't have a chance. She reached up, grabbed my shirt with both hands and fisted tightly, yanking me forward.

She was on fire.

Demanding and all hands.

She took charge and I let her, as she undid my fly and zipper, pulling my cock free.

Within seconds she had me pressed against her

just before shifting her hips and we both let out the most satisfied groans, sounding as if they were almost in sync.

"You feel so damn good," I praised her as I began to move my hips. With each thrust of my own she met me stroke for stroke.

We were both so lost in the moment that neither us were aware of what was going on around us until we heard the disgusted groans of both my brothers.

"What the hell, Jack?" Ryan barked.

"Will the two of you ever be able to keep your god-damned clothes on?" Noah added as I looked back to see both of them scramble back out of the barn.

I looked back toward my wife as she lay before me, her legs still wrapped around my waist, but she wore the most gorgeous smile.

"Bailey," I whispered as I reached out and trailed my finger along her lower lip. "I love you so much, baby."

"I love you too." She looked back at me with those big beautiful eyes of hers and gave me all I needed in that moment.

I always said I'd be perfectly content in my life if I never got married and had kids. I could be alone—hell, alone meant I had no one else to worry about but me.

Only now surrounded by my kids and my wife, I knew that was wrong because had I chosen to live that life alone, I would have missed out on the most amazing life a man could have.

I was a very lucky man.

Alena

"Hayden, please tell me you sent me some of Heather's new line, because I am wearing one of her fall line specials and it is absolutely amazing." I spun from side to side, looking at the way the red material covered my body.

I felt beautiful.

Something I was still struggling with after the birth of Nicolas only a few months ago. I was still trying so hard to get back to my pre-baby weight.

"Yes sweetie," Hayden assured me with a chuckle. "I have five of the same dress you're wearing and five of the longer style."

I felt all giddy inside, imagining one of the longer style on me next.

"You're having one of those moments, aren't you?" Hayden pulled me out of my daydream and I laughed.

"Yes I am," I said without hesitation. "Put a rush on them," I added just before hanging up to the sound of his arrogant laughter.

So I loved my clothes.

I found no harm in that.

What kind of store owner would I be if I didn't sample the merchandise prior to selling it?

I turned around at the sound of the door opening and was faced with one of the most beautiful visions.

My husband.

He held our son in a sling that was strapped to his chest, one arm resting on his back. The other arm hung at his side and the tiny little hand of our daughter held on tightly to her daddy's. And just behind Nora stood Austin.

There they all remained staring back at me, like I was their world.

Nothing, and I do mean nothing, made me feel more alive.

"Hi," I said, feeling my throat burn with such emotions.

"Hey mommy," Noah said as he sauntered toward me with the most gorgeous smile.

He still gave me goosebumps.

Nora released her daddy's hand as she stepped up to me and wrapped her arms around my legs.

"Hello sweet baby," I said, placing my hand to her head and smoothing back her hair. "How's your day been with daddy?"

I didn't expect much of an answer, because our little Nora was a quiet girl. But when she started bouncing up and down with excited squeals I couldn't stop myself from jumping around with her.

"Daddy played dollies," she said with a bright smile.

"Oh he did, did he?" I looked up at Noah and he winked.

I had a vision of my big strong man sitting alongside his daughter on the floor as he brushed a doll's hair and made little girl voice impressions.

"Yes, I did," Noah stated proudly.

My heart was full, so very full. I had the love of the most amazing man I'd ever met and three of the most beautiful children. I had a great family and supportive friends.

I'm not sure there was anything out there that

could ever make me happier than I already was. In fact I knew there wasn't. I already had way more than I could have ever hoped to have.

I reached out and placed my arms around my husband's neck and pulled him down to me, my lips pressed firmly to his. "You're amazing," I whispered. "And I love you so much."

"And we love you too."

Noah

"Mom," I hollered out as I entered the back door of her house. Within seconds that damn ugly ass dog she inherited from Trinity came barreling toward me, yapping and growling.

Why in the hell she took in this mutt is something I would never know, but she absolutely loved the thing.

The dog kept yapping and suddenly I regretted volunteering to clean the gutters.

"Where are my babies?" I spun around to face my mother as she came in from outside with remnants of leaves and whatever else the brown debris was that covered the rubber gloves she wore.

"Um they're at home with Alena, and what in hell is all over your hands?" I pointed toward the crap I was referring too and she held her hands up and twisted them from side to side.

"Oh," she said with a shrug. "I was cleaning the gutters."

What the hell?

"I told you I'd be over to do that." Damn woman was stubborn as shit. No wonder she and Chase's grandmother got along so well. They were both pigheaded.

"Well now you don't have to." She moved past me as she removed the gloves and bent down to pat her dog on the head. "You can get back in your truck and move your ass back home to pick up those babies. I'm needing a fix."

She smiled brightly.

"You two work too much and spend too little time together." She began to lecture. "Go home, get cleaned up, and bring me those little angels."

I looked at her with curiosity and she laughed.

"Take your wife to dinner, son, and me and my grandbabies will have a slumber party."

My mother had the biggest heart.

After my father passed she filled her life with her grandchildren every possible chance she could. She was the rock to our family

The one who held us together. She picked us up when we fell, kicked us in the ass when we needed to clear our minds, and loved each and every one of us so fiercely you often found yourself wondering how one person could have so much love to give.

"All right, Ma," I agreed as I offered her a kiss on her cheek before running off to do just as she asked.

That was another thing.

No one second-guessed Ma; she'd beat you with a broom if you even tried.

Olivia

"How you feeling?" Keeton asked as he sat

down the ginger ale and crackers on the bedside table. "Any better?"

I offered him a reassuring smile as I reached out and pulled him down onto the bed beside me.

"I'm better now," I said as I curled in closer to his body. "But do you know what would make me feel as close to perfect as possible?"

"You're already perfect." He gave me that loving look he gave me often, the one I adored.

"Thank you," I added before I continued. "But you tucked in bed beside me would help me forget that I just spent the last two hours with my head hovering over the garbage can."

Keeton crawled over me as he tucked his body in securely behind mine.

We lay in that position for some time before he spoke, a soft whisper against my ear. "I hate that you're sick, beautiful girl, but I love what's causing it."

I was as relaxed as he held me close, but I couldn't stop the smile that spread out over my face. "Me too," I confessed.

"We're gonna have a baby," Keeton whispered and all over again I got that excited, happy feeling I got the moment we saw the two pink lines on the test only a week ago.

"It's so strange to think about." I placed my hand over his, resting over the space that held our child. "There is a little us growing in there," I said almost dreamily.

"When are we gonna tell everyone?" he asked hopefully.

The guy was ready to rent space on the nearest

billboard and announce to everyone willing to listen that he and I were going to be parents.

During the entire time of waiting for that little stick to tell us yes or no, I was a nervous wreck. Biting my nails, tapping my foot. But not Keeton, he was all smiles as he hovered over the sink, staring down at the item that could forever change our future.

And the moment those lines appeared I didn't even get the chance to look before he spun around, hooting like he'd just won the lottery.

He picked me up, spun me around, and sang his praise of the gift he'd said I'd just given him.

"I think we should wait until Sunday dinner at Gran's house." I told him as I turned my head to look back over my shoulder, once again finding that happy grin of his.

I loved more than anything else to see him so happy.

Keeton had never had that loving family, and I was more than happy to share mine with him.

And now we were just adding yet another sweet little addition to the mix.

Keeton

"So we have some news." Suddenly all eyes were on me. I was nervous and I truly had no idea why. I'd been in the Sawyer family for years now. I'd been accepted and as far as I could tell all resistance had depleted.

After all, we were married now.

But all eating had stopped.

All conversation had ended.

And I was now on center stage.

"Don't leave us hanging," Bailey pushed and I shouldn't have been surprised. The woman was loud, crude, and never shy, and she had grown to become one of my most favorite people in this family.

I reached out from under the table and took Olivia's hand in my own, linking our fingers together. After Olivia and I shared a look of love, I looked back toward our family, Ryan in particular, and shared with them the best news I had ever been given in my life.

"Olivia and I just found out that she's pregnant." Ryan tried to keep a straight face because I knew the man didn't think his daughter and I shared a bed every night without actually touching one another, but this was just confirmation of the dirty things I did to his daughter.

"Daddy," Olivia warned and Jackson chuckled.

After a few more seconds of Ryan's glare, making me wonder if I should run and hide, he cracked. "I'm just playing, darlin'," he said with a laugh.

I watched with a knot in my stomach as he stood from his seat, walked around the table, and paused at my side. A tense moment passed before he reached out and held his hand out for mine.

Placing my palm against his, he gripped mine firmly and shook.

"Congratulations," he said.

"Thank you," I replied, finally feeling as if the weight of the world was no longer pressing down on my chest.

He then looked at his daughter. "My girl is gonna be a momma."

Within seconds she was up from the chair and in her dad's arms as he held her close and they shared a moment just between the two of them that the rest of us were lucky enough to experience.

Just another flash forward…

Olivia gave birth to a beautiful baby girl, who was named after her mother.

Claire Emilia Pearce.

Keeton was instantly wrapped around their little brown haired girl's finger.

Sweet little Claire would one day grow to be the very best friend of Corinne Marie Douglas, the daughter of Trinity and Chase Douglas.

The two would be become inseparable, surviving the torment from Liam, Chase and Trinity's sneaky son, who always looked for ways to gross out the younger girls every chance he got.

Author

s see where to start.
., as long as they come packing
d some excitement, some angst,
at make me fan my face, those are
too. I am an Illinois girl, born and
.ple and true, it honestly doesn't take
make me happy. I love the little things,
.uly mean the most. I may have a slight
.ction to my new Keurig, oh my, that thing is a
odsend. And so fast too. I have two children who truly are my very best friends; their faces never fail to put a smile on my face. I have been married to my husband for sixteen years and even though at times I want to beat him with a stick, I would never change the years we have had. We have learned and fallen, only to pick each other up, dust off the ache, and help each other make it right.

I am one of those authors that adore my fans—I love to hear from you. After all, it is because of each one of you that I continue to write. I look forward to you feedback.

Be sure to follow me to stay up to date on all my upcoming releases.

Facebook:
www.facebook.com/pages/Author-CA-Harms/354791947956151

Twitter:
https://twitter.com/Charms0814

Blog:
http://authorharms.blogspot.com/

Goodreads:
www.goodreads.com/author/show/6895633.C_A_Harms

Limitless Publishing:
http://www.limitlesspublishing.net/authors/c-a-harms/

Newsletter:
http://bit.ly/1xsgHCS

CPSIA information can be obtained
at www.ICGtesting.com
Printed in the USA
LVHW042158300420
654814LV00005B/1502

9 781640 349636